AARON EISCHEID

Scry For Help

A Novella of Grief

PARADIGMSHIFT
PRODUCTIONS

First published by Paradigm Shift Productions 2019

First edition

ISBN: 978-1-7334256-0-5

Cover art by Loren Greenblatt

This book was professionally typeset on Reedsy.
Find out more at reedsy.com

For Clive

When I had journeyed half of our life's
way,
I found myself within a shadowed
forest, for I had lost the path that does
not stray.
Ah, it is hard to speak of what it was,
that savage forest, dense and difficult,
which even in recall renews my fear:
so bitter—death is hardly more se-
vere!

DANTE ALIGHIERI, <u>THE DIVINE</u>
<u>COMEDY</u>

Contents

I

Kaleidoscopes & Shadow Men

Chapter 1

"**H**old still," Jamie might have said. Nate swore those were the words he saw formed yet they were muted upon delivery. He attempted to ask for repetition but struggled to find a single muscle, let alone his tongue or either of his lips, to do so.

Perched atop the toilet nearby, Jamie was peering at him through rising puffs of steam, silently drumming his fingers across the sketchpad in his lap. He was trying to convey annoyance. The way his face comically wrenched between a frown and a grin stifling a chuckle, however, came across more as adorably perturbed. The look was not unfamiliar to Nate. It had always meant SOMEONE was being uncooperative about SOMETHING.

About what this time around, though, vexed Nate. *Where even am I?*

But there was no time for puzzling. Impatient at just being gawked at, Jamie jabbed the pad forward. *"I said: HOLD STILL,"* he mouthed. *"You promised."*

Nate tried harder this time to strain his ears or at least make his eyes roll in their sockets (if anything to find out what he was doing to agitate Jamie) only to discover failure on all fronts. All the pieces of the present Moment were at incredible odds with one another.

An equally maddened air clouded over Nate. It vibrated with resonant rumbles as its pressure mounted. Nate perceived a creeping suffocation tighten against what he guessed to be his chest. The air was compressing into his essence, flattening him.

Suddenly, Jamie smirked without context and, before long, all out smiled. With what appeared to be a cheeky, *"Thank you,"* he turned his attentions away to a collection of watercolor paint supplies spread across the sink.

Nate observed the increasingly strange disconnect with profound confusion. Nothing on his part was done to appease his boyfriend yet here Jamie was moving on to rifle through paint brushes like everything was normal. Nate felt ignored and left behind. Like he was not even there. Stuck.

There rose the uncomfortable dawn: he had done nothing. He was helpless. And he was there…once. But no longer.

To be part of this Moment, a deep recess in his psyche icily informed him, *you must sacrifice your devices to be conscious; to be a disembodied fly pinned on the wall, affixed to the perspective we have chosen to leave you, with no kind regards for stopping. Or caring.*

The compromise was utterly distasteful. Nate nonetheless submitted because Jamie was once again staring at him, basking him with those inquisitive forest green eyes mounted perfectly equidistant above that naturally sculpted nose. They were staring simultaneously towards and through Nate seeking sights unknown with every innocent, glistening glance.

Jamie selected a long, spindly brush and clamped it between his teeth like Holly Golightly's cigarette holder. He scrutinized Nate with a keen once over. Then, he popped open the crusted lid of each pan, dabbed the parched brush bristles in a Mason jar of water and sopped up the desired pigment—all without looking. His heart knew the supplies. Dancing the brush against his cheek, Jamie pondered how to stroke it. His skin stained in tiny swatches.

Jamie paid them no mind. The chosen viridian shade accented his own irises to a marvelous degree. The green was just an extension of an already luminous piece born out of every hue in the palette.

Art had created Jamie. Jamie imitated art.

Ready to commence, Jamie puffed out of the corner of his mouth to clear the wispy tuft of bangs that always dangled down to obstruct his sightline. The poufy hairs were stubborn though and, also always, refused to budge. Too carefree to swat them, Jamie cheerily surrendered the battle and began to paint.

As deep artistic focus absorbed Jamie, Nate perceived the Moment he was inside shift curiously towards real time, slightly alleviating the pent-up pressure wall. From someplace rare, a gracious occasion was being quietly stolen to afford him the chance to be more flexible; to take more in and appreciate some.

Nate's nerve endings seized the opportunity to tell him his back was reclined along a curved surface that was slick, warm and wet. Phantom limbs tingled and floated listlessly elsewhere. His sight pored over every visible feature on Jamie's wiry late-twenty-something-year-old body, using all the imagination he could stir to fill in the remaining intimate details.

Jamie worked with confident, precise brushstrokes. Nate watched in awe as the handle bobbed up and down and side to side with purposeful pokes and prods. Whichever shape was being formed was being directed, impromptu, by an inspired genius. His genius.

My genius, Nate's thoughts managed to sigh into the mix.

Jamie mashed the brush along his tee shirt between dyes of cleanses past. It was time to switch colors. Jamie quickly swished the brush in the water, the rest of the green spiraling off in tendril-like strands that curled about the jar. He swabbed at another color while behind him, up in the corner of the room—

The barricade slammed back. In it skulked dread. The mighty feeling reached straight out for Nate's throat.

What the...? How? This is impossible, his thoughts choked.

—the corner spat plaster. Spidery threads of viridian pooled from the resulting cracks, crawling out of them in vines. The wall itself wavered as if it were being washed away or...

...painted over?

Coming back to Jamie, Nate's aura was jarred. The *artiste's* actions had turned hasty and shuddery. He was already changing colors again. Peachy flesh tone collided with the green in the water jar and spurt out a geyser.

This time from the floor.

Something was wrong, very wrong. The helplessness returned to overcome Nate. The Moment was swiftly trying to regain control.

Jamie lifted his pad to completely obscure his face. He feverishly stabbed the brush at every pan before he arched it high then plunged it down to the jar. He swirled it around and around...

...and around...and around...

…faster and faster…

…until the little whirling vortex stripped the pigments of their vibrancy and blended them to a murky, soulless gray.

What was leeched discarded itself in a cascade over Jamie. What was now devoid amassed behind him and splashed the walls. The already buckling façade started to bend and warp upon itself.

Amid the chaotic fugue, a kaleidoscopic form akin to Jamie had stood up: an abstracted body of water-colored flesh. In its hand was the sketchpad with the unrevealed, finished painting wedged inside. The kaleidoscope nodded to Nate and delivered a timid, one-handed wave bye-bye.

When, dramatically, it seized up in knots.

The pressure in the Moment warbled. The strange form quaked. Out of the kaleidoscope's back peeled a foot-like growth that, trailed by stringy, stick figure appendages, stepped down and bore a crooked, black as midnight shadow man.

The entrance drew shrill, wailing screams that blasted Nate's eardrums.

The shadow man split from its host and spread its shoulders, rolling with inaudible laughter at something insanely funny. The screaming ceased after the last laugh. It too waved at Nate—a mischievous hello—before it snatched the heaving kaleidoscope's sketchpad and stole for the door.

Everything happened so fast. Nate could not contemplate who the shadow man was. The only thing he could blurrily discern was where it bolted: the adjoining hallway.

No.

The crooked progeny began to shred apart from the inside-out, hoisting two tall, oblong objects.

No!

Suitcases.

The door slammed. There was a pause. Three drawn, booming thuds echoed outside. Silence then sealed the room and sense no longer mattered.

Jamie's abstraction abruptly materialized before Nate, rocking on the edge of what the last lingering pocket of rationality only now made out as the bathtub Nate was sunken into this whole time. The blush pinks and jaunty yellows on Jamie's kaleidoscopic face lent amazing optimism to the bizarre scene. But the overflowing sadness of evening blues and royal purples in and around its pouting lips betrayed a notion that the worst was yet to come. Swinging around towards the invisible bathwater, it unfurled its arms like angels' wings and lithely slid its colorful nakedness onto Nate's lap to embrace him.

Hissing streams of static broke the silence. Violent splotches began to banish the Moment's backdrop.

The kaleidoscope proffered a kiss and leaned in, so closely, to give it.

The Moment, however, was merciless. Torrential water flooded in and drowned everything—the grays, the colors, the Jamie—in complete, infinite darkness.

And cold.

So much cold.

Chapter 2

Nate stood in the shower, numb and taut, as needle-like streams of frigid water roared out of the head and stung his face. He clenched the dial in one trembling fist while the other hand held his ground against the assault by palming the slippery tile. All was dark.

Three drawn, booming thuds echoed outside.

The Moment kept ebbing and flowing from the same points in his head since its first appearance four nights ago.

BOOM to **black**. BOOM to **black**. BOOM to **black**.

Like an obnoxiously baiting headache. Further dastardly was how fragments continued to go missing along the way no matter how hard Nate racked his brain to replay it in full or even keep a few precious bits in focus. The Moment, bred in REM, could not have lasted more than, say, two or three minutes. Memory, even as young as his, though, was unable to keep up with the pieces falling by the damnable wayside this vivid brand of dreams frequently and frustratingly courted.

His only choice was to try and freeze the lingering frames; to solidify them in his bank and ice away their feelings so everything, from now 'til forever, would be picture perfect.

Nate tugged the dial. The temperature plummeted to a dangerous low. He tensely sucked his breath as subzero scored his goose-fleshed skin. Purplish spots danced in the dark and began to spin, one by one, in hypnotic, concentric symmetry along his eyelids. Bright spikes of yellow and white jaggedly bled out the spots' borders as frost tickled Nate's skull. In the middle of their madcap whirl wobbled lines flailing to bond into something cohesive.

Come back, Nate's brain begged the kaleidoscope. *You can do it, my dream.*

The lines drew erect, burning bright...growing closer.

BOOM.

Nate's lungs sputtered.

BOOM.

His eyes flew open.

BOOM.

His attentions were wrested back.

Back to the bathroom.

Nate cut off the shower with a knee to the dial. He shivered blankly. The curtain tapped against the edge of the tub. Nate pondered it: *could this be a veil?*

A tiny pressure built in his forehead as he reached, slowly, for the curtain. Just to see if...

He snapped the curtain aside. He gasped...then sighed, disappointed.

The bathroom was empty. Absent of color. Nobody on the toilet. Nothing at all changed.

Three gentle knocks and a man's voice called from outside, "Nate? Did you hear me?"

Nate scowled. He wasn't alone. At least, not with anyone that mattered right now.

"Hey man," the voice pled, "please answer me. Just say you're in there and alright."

Nate immodestly draped a towel around his waist and answered the door. It was Max, his scruffy downstairs neighbor, dressed in his Sunday finest with an old Kodak draped about his neck. Nate thought he had told Max earlier to fuck off and now silently chastised himself for neglecting to relay the message properly. To make matters worse, Max had brought and was cradling his marauding alley calico, Mocha. Two annoyances for the price of one.

Oblivious to any misdeed, Max nonetheless proceeded softly, "Sorry if I startled you. You were in there a while—God you are red," he peered at Nate's numbed flesh, but the latter expressed no concern so he continued, "Anyway, our ride's downstairs. I got him to wait a few extra minutes so we aren't late for—"

Fed up already with listening, Nate shoved past and stormed up the stairs to the bedroom.

Mocha hissed at the forceful gesture. Max shushed her and finished his sentence to no one in particular, "—for the funeral."

Max paused and waited several long minutes in silence for Nate to return from upstairs. He kissed his kitty on the forehead. Mocha purred appreciatively, needing love, too, on this sad, solemn day.

II

The Lucid Paradox

Chapter 3

The next day, Wednesday, Nate, blank and unrested, lied in his office swivel chair. A potently ill-mixed blend of brain chemistry injected little agency to his cognizant limbs sprawled out in limp-noodle repose. Motivation, drive and productivity were nowhere near reasonable levels to try and overcome these deficiencies. Whether Nate cared about this or not was not a factor in the equation. From about noon 'til now, close to shift's end, his heart was solely invested in simply being adrift and awash in the world's greatest natural drug: apathy.

Staring at the ceiling, he was wishing nothing had ever left at all.

Around four o' clock, a tinny melody rose among the thousand peaks and valleys of the white stucco. It rang in terse notes, never in the same place twice. Nate followed each note with a glazed, fixated stare in an attempt to ascertain their origin. Their faintness indicated a journey from someplace far away but, with the right concentration, were not out of reach.

As the melody persisted, though, a worrisome hunch started worming about Nate's stuporous preoccupation. The ceiling, deceivingly bland, was pocked with microscopic shadows nestled within said stucco's valleys. In them, his hunch felt, was something else being held back behind the rings, which could explain their randomization.

Nate's thoughts raced to dredge up all they knew about paint and its ways and inquired of the troubling theory:

If white light scientifically reflects all wavelengths in the prism off of white paint, why empirically would any appear to be missing? Because when light does not cast in all directions and creates blackness colors are—

—*absorbed! That must be it,* Nate became convinced. *The chimes were of one or more captive forms of light calling me, wanting out.*

To be with me.

Nate's focus deepened, his new goal to will the stucco into tweezing itself apart and let loose what he was positive yearned to be free. What right did this barrier (or anything) have to hoard away such beauty?

But the ceiling was stubborn and Nate's hopes dwindled as it remained in stasis while the notes just kept on ringing,

ringing,

ringing.

"Psst," a feminine whisper interjected, "your phone is ringing."

Nate jolted up and coughed on the pool of spittle that had built up in his gawking mouth. The indicator bulb on his cubicle's direct line was flashing in a tizzy. Nate hastily brushed the drool off onto his hand and lunged to answer the call. The drool's musty scent made him cringe as he brought the receiver to his ear.

"Strotman Incorporated Accounts Receivable, this is Nathan, how may I assist you," Nate greeted in politely scripted tone while futilely trying to transfer the bodily fluids to his dress shirt. A low, wordless hum was the initial response. Nate waited a moment in case it was some sort of signal delay only to find the whine stayed on the line. Drawn out and peculiarly mannered, it made Nate stammer his follow-up, "Account—acc—cc—hello?"

"Zzz pff sss mwarrrrr," mechanical garble patched through, hissing into Nate's ear; passing along the most titillating patch of the canal. The receiver quivered in his hand, instantly seduced enough by the robotic gibberish not to hang up. *"Eeeevoice purrrr maahhhhh,"* more crackled out, silencing a second, then loudly exclaiming, *"I KNOWWWWWW."*

Nate slammed the phone down. His hairs prickled straight on end. *Son of a bitch thinks he knows what?!* He peered panicked at the ceiling and scowled suspiciously. The way the mysterious voice aimed its words, the way it sent shivers through him, seemed rather…*shadowy.*

There was a muffled ring and subsequent greeting in the cubicle next door.

"Psst," the feminine whisper returned behind Nate, "you have a phone call."

Nate swiveled around to see his newbie Accounts Payable neighbor Janelle flopping a cheery wave at him. Or perhaps it was her sweater. Nate could not tell. She was wearing that kind of oversized knit one that, when you gesture, it gestures bigger, like it was trying to tell you just how cozy an article of clothing it really was. She nonetheless wore the ensemble well, complemented by frizzy curls, ebony skin and an ebullient grin she no doubt gave to friend and strangers alike. Unfortunately, Nate hadn't a clue of what to do for her in the moment.

Sensing this, she gladly took the lead, "It's Mr. Powers from the Grand Hotel downtown, wants status on the finalized invoice for the housekeeping amenity order he placed. He apologizes for the spotty connection."

Nate nodded and stuttered, frozen like an idiot.

"Don't worry," Janelle winked it off, "I'll take a message." She slid back to her side. "Good afternoon, Mr. Powers, I sincerely appreciate your patience. Accounts Receivable is currently unavailable but I will be more than happy to assist. Now…"

Nate slumped over his desk, listening to the conversation through cradled hands.

What the fuck is going on, he mentally bemoaned. There were no details of the past hours he could instantaneously recollect nor was he able to develop any fathomable explanation for his headspace. He just knew he was dazed beyond reason and drained as all Hell.

Minutes later, Janelle thumbed a Post-It to his wall and waved an equally floppy, sweet bye-bye. Nate snatched up the note and slapped it on his computer monitor. Leaning in to read Janelle's curly cursive pass-on, the vivacious pink shade of the Post-It struck a familiar chord and gave Nate pause. He twisted around to look outside his cubicle.

The office was uneventful, colleagues of every variety gliding past, noses stuck in their own business of files or cell phones. All blasé and blah, nobody presented much personality or style. Just the Post-It. The note written on it was whatever. It was the special, glowing background hue Nate was missing and could find nothing of compare in the workplace.

—nor will you at home, remember, until you pick it up from the police station—

Nate swallowed hard and leapt back to his keyboard, hastily clacking an email to Mr. Powers as *what the fuck is going on* surged back in spades. He remembered the haze of awakening this morning and the serious urge to call off. The bites of rent and other recent expenses out of his budget, however, resolutely convinced him to come in.

—the officer said you HAVE to stop in today, no exceptions. Do you think they know—

Nate stopped typing to proofread his e-mail and realized the thing was a jumbled mess.

—everything's a jumbled mess—

He backspaced an entire paragraph with his eyes closed, shoveling silence over his nagging internal monologue. Burying the rising anxiety in busy work served as further rationale for being at the office. He did not want to stare at the ceiling anymore or be snapped out of aimless dazes that came attached with sensations and reminders.

He just wanted to quickly tidy the mess of this e-mail and get money out of Mr. Powers.

Perfected soon after, Nate sent the e-mail off and clicked through the rest of his inbox for anything else to respond to or engage in. He fidgeted his legs back and forth, coming up empty. There was always the desk to rearrange. Or the phone would ring and, this time, he would not disconnect and have a nice, long chat! Plenty of occupiable options were around.

Just don't think, he went ahead and thought anyway. Nate grit his teeth at the irony.

The short path to five o' clock was going to be an excruciating one.

Chapter 4

Sitting in the hideous, government-sanctioned, bargain-basement chair of the Downtown Chicago police precinct was like sitting on a slab straight out of a hospital morgue. Cold, metal and out of whack, if years in the office swivel didn't murder Nate's spine, a little longer in this chair would. At a desk smack dab in the middle of the department, this was pushing aside many situations to rank as one of the most disquieting moments of Nate's life. He kept his eyes down to avoid catching the glare of passerby crooks in cuffs and officers whose looks are perpetually out to arrest you. The only thing he paid attention to were the mad chants of brutality protestors outside.

He empathized with their sense of despair and wholeheartedly supported their cause. Police stations were not built for happiness. Though he had never personally experienced what they decried, he understood the lunacy of the institution despite the foundation it stood on. If it were not for his own selfish reasons, he would be outside with them shutting the whole thing down.

Which brought him back to Officer Burgundy, the assigned cop taking her sweet time on the clerical mumbo jumbo Nate had been so urgently summoned in for. He watched her write on a clipboard with one hand while the other tapped crimson-emblazoned fingernails across the desk's cheap particle board. Nate would have questioned the longevity of his wait. The way Burgundy stiffly pursed her analogously painted lips, though, enforced every possible measure of restraint.

Finally, after a roughly awkward half hour, Officer Burgundy spun the clipboard around and slid it to him. "Sign here," she ordered, dropping her pen over the dotted line at the bottom.

Nate picked up the pen and examined it. What she handed over, and what he saw she wrote her entire report in, contained blood red ink.

"Really," Nate bravely sassed.

Officer Burgundy replied, unfazed, "Really. Red's an important color. Essential." She leaned forward, distinctive features outside of her lips oddly masked by her cap, and inquired with a serpent's smile, "Does that bother you?"

Nate shook his head and said, "No, I just find it inappropriate given the circumstances." He scrawled his signature and shoved the clipboard back at her.

She caught it gleefully and stowed it in her desk. Then did nothing.

Nate furrowed his brow and asked, "Can I just have what I came for?"

The Officer smirked and cocked her head. "It does bother you," she toyed. "I can sense a perp's insides tensing from a mile away. And you look positively spring-loaded."

Nate lost all feeling in his person.

Officer Burgundy chuckled, then produced a cardboard box from under her desk and passed it to Nate. "Here," she said. "I honestly don't think you want it but you are going to have to have it as we are not a citizen's storage locker."

21

Nate begrudgingly hugged the box to his chest and muttered, "Thank you, Officer."

"You're welcome," she cooed with sick, treacly relish before brandishing her index finger for him to wait just a wee bit longer. She yanked open her drawer and grabbed a thick manila envelope. She handed it to Nate and, rapping her nails for emphasis, added, "It is my pleasure to serve you...with the accident report you also 'forgot' to pick up."

* * *

Jamie left the classroom of color saturated canvasses sporting a jovial grin. Clenched in his armpit were his precious leather satchel and a mystery work he had created within. His kinetic hands were miming paint strokes as he excitedly exchanged words with an equally impassioned female student walking alongside. They were talking the shared language of artists about technique, experimentation and history.

The indefatigable rate at which it all tumbled out of Jamie was amazing. An entire state's drive, a Master's seminar and then a beginner's course audit: total breeze. There was still plenty of openness left in his schedule to seamlessly blend in with these undergrad strangers he was seven-some-years removed from as well as convert them into fast friends.

Stopping in the hall, Jamie turned, his eyes brimming like two hazel saucers, and waved cutely to the accompaniment who had waited so patiently for him on the bench outside the class. Jamie pointed up a 'One minute' finger and went back to the girl. She, the amateur, had obviously asked a question that he, the humble expert, decided to make a teachable moment.

Jamie knelt down and motioned for the girl to join him as the stash under his arms spilled to the floor. Jamie rummaged both his paint pan and a brush out from his satchel and turned over a random leaflet to use as drawing paper. The brush, though, was bone dry. Jamie twisted about to discover a water source in a nearby drinking fountain. He arched into a wondrous back bend, then reached and slapped the fountain for a shot of water. The obstacle cleared, he snapped back and moistened some pigment.

Jamie chased up his bangs with a pouf of air and demonstratively flicked his brush across the paper. The girl watched intently. She repeated the rudimentary motion with her hand and nodded that she got it but Jamie sweetly tut-tutted. He would not allow the lesson to stop there. He cupped her hand and guided her into the stroke. The persistence became practice as he let go. Only then, on her own, did the girl understand and blushed her appreciation for the selfless transferral of talent. Looking at her watch, the girl pointed out the time and indicated she had to run. She continued to thank and wave as she walked away, sincerely hoping she would see Jamie around.

More minutes passed as the brushstroke kept Jamie beguiled on his knees. He was dreaming: dreaming he was flowing with the paint trails as they bled, wondering where the directions of them all led. He would be like this all day because unrealized work equaled unsatisfactory work, even if it was randomized for educational benefit.

He was the perfect dream boy. That's why he was here visiting this school. He could study his dreams for two years with semester breaks and holidays to visit home in between. According to the pamphlets Jamie's gentleman accompaniment began to re-read, however, the program was naturally intensive and suggested the chances of those visits would grow slim as time went on.

And time had already been overrun by ten drawn minutes when the increasingly fidgety accompaniment approached Jamie from the bench to nudge him away from his art.

Jamie looked up and put an 'Oops' hand over his mouth. He quickly gathered up his things and sprung to his feet. Wrapping a flirty, grateful hug around his gentleman's waist, he purred something about being a saint then shoved off into a distracted, jagged walk down the hall. He clasped his things to his chest like a new kid in town. He was still dreaming, now about this place. About liking it...

...and picturing his chance to part of it.

Jamie swooped over to a social event calendar tacked to a bulletin board and perused it and the surrounding flyers of the various available mingling options. He took a snapshot of an upcoming classic movie night series that fell within his potential residency. There were others: intramural sports teams, painting and wine pairing sessions, an online course promotion.

About that last one, Jamie's accompaniment made the targeted joke about just doing everything from home.

Jamie sagged and pivoted, sweeping nonplussed 'Fuck you' eyes at the sarcasm. He shuffled away wounded, his tennis shoes squeaking on the vinyl tiles. He hugged his chest tighter. For all his excitement, parting ways was no picnic for him either.

The accompaniment put a conciliatory hand on Jamie's shoulder. Jamie patted it and glanced over. He said, "I'll make sure the RA in the dorm gives me permission for you to stay the night. Then we'll put a do not disturb sock on the door so everyone will know Nate's over. Okay?"

Game, set, match. The decision was made.

"C'mon," Jamie beckoned, "we'll make the rest quick so we won't have to drive back in the dark. Nobody likes that." He poufed his bangs and headed for the door that exited to campus.

There was no exit. The door never opened. And Jamie was out of *sight.*

All the students in the hall stopped and stared at the ground. The veins in their foreheads bulged as their pallor went white as sheets. They gaped like they had just seen the future erased before their very eyes. Like it had been stolen without warning. Like every drop of bright and promising potential they were told they had was suddenly rendered as unrealized and unsatisfactory as an unfinished work; snuffed out and dissolved into a blank, petrifying landscape, never to be heard from ever, ever again.

* * *

Sparks rocketed off the 'el' track rails as the green line screeched out of Downtown to the West Loop. Squashed in a sweaty herd, the commuting throng elbowed one another for balance in the careening car. Briefcases and backpacks slung casually about as everyone used their baggage as additional tools to prioritize their personal space over each other's.

Stuck between a preppy college kid and overdressed Financial District crony, Nate cupped his belonging, the box, like a precious relic. Every few minutes the train arrived at a station and whooshed its doors open to alleviate the crowding. The herd would stampede their home platform, their disorderly exits jamming the doors back open whenever they tried to close. Arriving at the area's most popular station, the jam was so intense it brought the commute to a full stop.

Antsy, Nate counted how many more stops to go as the masses figured out how to flow.

One.

The skin of his palms itched from the dry cardboard. Speculation of the box's contents made the itch burn. The manila envelope folded in Nate's coat pocket wove a worried nausea tightly around his digestive organs (the *femme fatale* cop had certainly nailed that internal observation; oh, how she'd be grinning) that the post office might shutter for the day before the jam ended.

"Clear the doors please, doors ARE closing," the conductor informed over the intercom and delivered on that promise.

Nate's station finally showed up and he sprinted past anyone in his way. He made the post office in the nick of time. He scribbled a delivery address on the envelope—no return one—then paid the postage with a wad of bills and ran out before the clerk could inquire if anything liquid, fragile or perishable was inside.

The errand done, Nate dashed with spare spurts of energy to his final destination that was awaiting three unevenly paved blocks over and two behemoth stair flights up.

* * *

The Loft emitted a thirsty sigh as the fresh air of the building's foyer rushed upstairs and through the burst-open front door. A welcome mat of long shadows rolled out for its dear lessee, Nate, as he breathlessly arrived home.

Bypassing the hook on the wall, Nate clattered his keys to the floor and hastily latched the door behind him. He fumbled for the broom closet. The Loft hid few things well and Nate desperately needed to stash the box that was about to sear his hands off. He found the closet handle and pried open the folding doors. Having to shove aside the broom, mop and Dirt Devil, Nate wedged the box in with the cleaning supplies and sealed them all up.

The relief expelled Nate's last sense of urgency for the day. He shimmied off his coat and swayed into the bathroom, illuminating the fixture above the sink. In the dim light, he washed his hands of the sweat and the papery grit. The burn subsided. He wiped his hands on the same patch of shirt where his drool had earlier dried and caught his reflection in the act. The mirror image was a sucker punch to the gut: so haggard and beleaguered.

"Don't you have anything better to show me," Nate whined at the mirror. He slouched down to the sink to look away and swore in streams.

Tap-tap.

Nate stopped cursing and perked his ears.

Tap-tap.

He peeked out the bathroom. The Loft was shrouded in night, no one else around. It was likely one of the many architectural moans and groans this old building—

TAP TAP TAP.

It came from the broom closet.

Nate toppled onto his rear. Shivering, he stared the closet door down across the long shadows he noticed The Loft had not rolled back, but made longer.

TAP!

The door bowed. Nate flinched. He regretted bringing the damnable box home.

I should have just mailed you too.

He waited for another sound that never came.

Nate pulled himself up, wiped out, sure to pass out if he did not just go to sleep. *Shit.* That meant passing the closet to get to the bedroom. *Shit!* He mulled over a path. *Turn on the hall light. Run by. Do. Not. Look.* There were options, he knew. He just had to do them.

A single foot got out the bathroom door.

TAP TAP TAP TAP TAP, erupted from the closet!

The lynchpin holding Nate's—

— *"positively spring loaded," Officer Burgundy sneered—*

—guts together popped loose. He doubled over the toilet and splat days' worth of vomit around the bowl.

Chapter 5

L inc floated an offer across the space, "Do you want *me* to open the box?"

Nate, his back turned on the space, received the inquiry in one ear and fed it out the other through the horizontal designer blinds. The offer successfully discarded, Nate resumed his attentions on the dot-sized elementary school children below the community center scattering into formation to play soccer.

He wondered how the children would respond to the question being dropped on them. They'd probably believe they were in for some sort of present, youthfully unaware of the possibilities that surrounded opening Pandora-esque boxes. If they really knew what was best they would kick the notion out of bounds with their ball.

"I'm not sure I *should*," Linc persisted. "Right now, you'll feel better if I did. Imagine, however, if *you* embrace the major step of having it here and open it. Penny for your thoughts?"

A whistle blew. Nate cocked his head and watched the checkerboard-shirted referee jog to mediate two players who apparently cried foul. Both were pushing and shoving over who tripped who.

"You wanna bring it back up here, Nate," Linc requested with a rap of the pen against their notepad. Nate brought only his face. So, Linc pointedly added, "I've watched a lot of those games from here. They're actually pretty good. Funny thing I've learned though is that the players already know how to sort out their quarrels. They just want the grown up to come in and make it easier to absolve them of any responsibility. They're kids, after all, that's how they act. But that's not how you do, right?"

The therapist always managed to lob acute truth barbs into their client's side with the most adroit professionalism. Stung, Nate flopped the rest of himself petulantly back onto the sofa. He wrung his knuckles, wordless and downcast.

"Deep breath, Nate. My intent's not to belittle. We trust each other more than that," Linc patiently assured, excising the stinger with their measured tone. Their native-Kentuckian twanged through and sutured the wound with Southern charm, "You're just flutterin' a lot like a hummin'bird and all I wanna do is talk. Let's meet at the usual place for now."

Nate twitched a wan grin. That gentility. It so effortlessly created and cemented the duos' simpatico from the start. Linc's brand of hospitality transported you to a sunny veranda where you lounged, sipping mint juleps, and traded witticisms amid the throes of real, honest to God conversation. It was a welcoming, obliging place Nate enjoyed traveling to but was having a real hard time reaching now.

A cursory glance at the tasteful end table situated between them made Nate's heart skip a beat. Joining Linc potentially meant bringing along the box perched atop.

In the grand scheme of boxes nothing superficially made this particular box stand out from the pack. Corrugated cardboard packaging comprised every side, every panel, and every flap.

The folds were prim. The tape job perfect. Its originator's stamp was the same generic company who killed all the same forests to assemble this box and the generations of boxes before it. Their sole, marketed purpose were for them to all sit, agape, for the masses to come and feed things they wanted suffocated until they felt compelled to unpack and resuscitate them back to life.

Misery herself packed this box.

"C'mon," Linc coaxed Nate from the usual place. "I'm here. Only me."

Nate swallowed hard and reared his head, instantly relieved when he found Linc waiting for him informally cross-legged in their chair. No pen and pad. No meeting room. No box.

Just the two of them basking in the sunshine. They each took a moment to soak it up.

Linc's icebreaker was simple but kind, "Hello, friend."

Nate's was shy and muted, "Hi."

"How you feelin'?"

"Been better."

"Understandable. Past three weeks you've been a lot more reserved."

"Have I?"

"Yup. Been missing our spirited discussions."

"Sorry, I, uh, don't remember."

"What do you remember?"

"Um," Nate paused. He squinted beyond Linc as if, somehow, the answer lied somewhere over their shoulder. Out of the beyond rumbled a sonic undercurrent that began on the horizon and snaked its way up to and around Nate's temples where it stirred up a pulsating headache. Suddenly, he gasped and, in his eyes, welled heavy, crestfallen tears.

Linc leaned in and prodded him, alarmed.

Nate turned to Linc genuinely confused and asked, "It's been three weeks?"

Linc fell along with Nate. Their prod opened to a warm, comforting hand on his knee.

Nate squeezed his eyes. He refused to cry. *When did the world end?* he asked himself.

"Nate, it's ok. Whatever you are feelin': it's normal. You're not alone. Let it out slowly. Guide me through it."

Nate shook his head, his eyes still squeezed.

"You mentioned to me the first session after the burial that you did something special together the last night. Why don't you tell me about that? Tell me about something special."

The headache intensified, the prompts uncoiling—*black as midnight*—recollections threatening to—*bolt out*—and vanish—*into the adjoining*—

"Why, were things not right? Were you both still fightin' up until he left? Nate?"

"NO," Nate sputtered, "that night it was all over." Linc wisely backed off to listen. "There wasn't anything left to fight about. He bought the suitcases. He kept the suitcases open. He packed the suitcases. Put them in the hall...that was it. He wouldn't let me fight anymore." Nate stopped to gnaw his nails before continuing mid-chew, "So, I did. I stopped. I stopped it all for him. All I ever did was for...I don't know...can we talk about something else?!"

Rays of sunshine high above fizzled out one by one, darkening the veranda. Dry rustling of cardboard scraped on wood.

"Absolutely, darlin'," Linc cooed with exaggerated lilt, "but less talkin' more openin'."

That was not Linc, Nate shuddered. *We are no longer on the veranda.*

A third party had indeed joined. The box on the end table materialized betwixt them and shifted on its own axis to face Nate.

Nate looked up at a suspect version of Linc sitting stiff-legged in a straight-backed sliding chair in the Therapy Center's waiting room. Nate, also in such a chair and the same, new place, twisted to look towards the space where his current appointment was being held. The rumbling undercurrent maintained, the headache it sprang throbbed.

What Nate saw in the room had him terribly bothered.

Nate turned to the strange Linc. "Do you feel it too," he asked them, "the strings yanking us around? Like an…elsewhere is trying to puppet us? I think that is the *spirited* discussion we're missing."

Linc gave a curt, non-committal nod.

Nate assumed it was not in their professional interest to buy into suggestions of the abstract unknown even if they appeared to be momentarily part of it themselves. So, Nate elaborated, "I feel it every day. This state I'm in, I guess I'll say. It's like a thick, dense haze that something's actively trying to emerge from. Multiple things. One's packed in this box. Others are in the ceiling or wherever. They all pervade my thoughts. I get so sick and tired."

"Does it have to be something horrible emerging from the haze? Could be something wonderful that you never expected. Maybe you just have to be more open to the experience."

Nate bowed his head.

"Let's see if you are," Linc whispered and, in the blink of an eye, vanished.

The rumbling undercurrent faded. Nate twisted back to what

bothered him in the space: he was watching himself through the doorway. His self was confronting the box. Reaching to open it, his self scraped up the first bits of tape from the edges and then clasped the sides, edging towards the flaps. In the waiting room, Nate waited with breathless awe.

When a whistle blew. *Shrill, wailing screams blasted—*

Nate, back in the space, recoiled from the box and leapt off the sofa towards the window and saw the referee down below running to settle another quarrel for the children. Nate ran his hands along the blinds to confirm they were real, that this was actually the space. He was not so sure. Defeated, he said to Linc, their usual selves in their armchair, "No. I can't do it. There's no need to do this."

Linc rose up and attempted to placate, "Nate, calm down, you are safe here, you are so close—"

"I'm serious, Linc! There is nothing I need to see in that box. Not all boxes need to be opened. Sometimes they just need to stay sealed up in a closet for moths to nibble on. Who knows if that red lipped civil servant actually gave me anything in the first place!"

"We're not here drawin' the existential paradox of if you don't open the box and look at its contents, was there ever actually anythin' inside," Linc retorted.

"But it is the paradox of being lucid in the middle of the worst dream that I can't wake up from. Reality at large feels like a disjointed puzzle and I'm not holding all the pieces. I don't know who is who, where is where, or what is doing the separating." He gestured towards the waiting room. "Weren't you just there with me mostly agreeing?"

"Was I where—what?"

Nate, frustrated, tossed up his arms.

"If you are referring to moments ago us investigatin' that box," Linc said. Nate nodded hopefully. Linc took up their therapist effects anew with rapid, nervous clicks of the pen and decided, "I'm not sure what I was seeing there with you. However, I do strongly empathize your incredible discomfort." They clapped their chest. "In here hurts. Grief manifests a million ways."

Incredulous, Nate scoffed, "Oh great, platitudes."

"I'm just trying to help make sense. There's no right way or process to mourning but there's definitely a wrong one. I sincerely don't want you walkin' the path where it forks off to everything hittin' you at once and doing way more harm. That's real. That's the hurt."

Nate leaned over the couch. It was his brain's turn to feel spring loaded.

Linc wanted to hold him. They implored, "Please, Nate, listen. You did the day after you heard the news. You notified the family and the friends. You did the funeral for him to rest in peace. Time to connect and do the rest."

Nate muttered gravely, "Linc, there's a few important things I failed to mention."

Linc poised their pen.

Nate paused. He stood up straight and shuffled about the carpet. "It's what were we talking about when I first got here. We kind of left that dangling...what was it?"

Linc did not even consult their notes. They took the evasive bait and deadpanned, "Your day. You were telling me about your work day."

Nate pointed an affirmative index finger. "That's right," he exclaimed. "Yeah, yeah. Work's been nonstop lately which you know would seem a strain on me but it's actually a wonderful feeling because productivity really energizes you and gives you

35

that feeling of accomplishment to show your bosses…"

Fifteen minutes later: *beep-beep. Beep-beep.*

"Oh shoot," Nate said theatrically to the clock. "I ran the time, didn't I?"

Linc frowned and mustered a chipper, "Next week?"

"I'll call you," Nate replied again with the index finger and darted out, nearly forgetting the box.

III

Spiritual Centrifuge

Chapter 6

Nate marked the weeks' worth of texts from Maggie 'READ'

Hey 9/2 12:35am

hey? 9/3 5:02am

We need to talk 9/7 2:14pm

Plz call me 9/7 2:15pm

I got ur mail 9/17 4:21pm

WTF NATE?!?! 9/17 4:21pm

First the silent treatment now this 9/17 4:33pm

U Heartless Asshole 9/26 11:07pm

and swiped them left to archived oblivion. Other threads of idle digital chatter stayed bold and ignored as the cell phone was silenced and flung to the bed. Responding to her, let alone random contacts, was by far Nate's lowest priority. If anyone texted again he would seriously consider skipping out on the next phone bill. Teach them all a lesson.

The idea necessitated more wine. Nate replenished his half-empty glass of Merlot back to brimming and then, as with all tipsy notions, forgot about it entirely as he leaned against the wooden railing built along the lofted bedroom overlooking the den. He gazed o'er the desolate landscape of empty furniture and—*what'd the listing call it?*—modern minimalism.

"Invest in the rapidly growing mix of urban bohemia," Nate declared, sarcastically paraphrasing the leasing agents' pitch. He knocked back a chug. "Enjoy the vast, wide windows; remove yourself from the noise of the street and your neighbors and be free—" Chug. "—be free to create whatever you desire in honest, blissful solitude."

Sip.

Just how much of that money was invested into semantics versus real estate was up for debate.

The Loft came built with a lived-in feel that palpably aged as its eras as a structure wore on. It was converted from a family of warehouses whose lineage traced all the way back to Chicago's chaotic and fast-paced Gilded Age, upon which this industrious West-Side had originally been founded. The vintage, heavy metal door locks circa 1970 hailed from when the place was a leather shoe factory. You could still track the faint scent of tanning in the creaky old floorboards; sweat and rawhide forever sealed in layered coats of wood stain. The dual trio of windows, upstairs and down, were honestly remarkable. They stretched floor to ceiling, letting in every radiant burst of the rising dawn and each glimmer of twilight shade. They wore their age too: every slightest bluster rattled the old glass panes in the misaligned window frames.

All in all, The Loft's distinctive austerity made it worth the while. Jamie was the artist and this was his blank canvas. He had felt the inclinations for craftsmanship the moment he walked in. He practically twirled at the abundance of studio space up in the lofted portion with room still left over for a king-sized bed (he preferred to sleep sprawling). Plus, there were stainless steel appliances, a granite kitchen island and reasonably updated plumbing. There was nothing to lose! Nate had picked up the lease without hesitation and it was theirs.

Nate never pictured being the sole resident. He had barely chosen a single decorative element out himself. It was almost always a joint decision. Most everything Nate did was with him.

Most everything I did was for him. The pronoun kept repeating. *Him. Him. HIM!*

"Jamie," Nate exhaled, freeing the name from his thoughts like it was brand new. The second time, he cried it, "JAMIE!"

The Loft, barren, creaky and rattling, absorbed the name calling without the slightest of echoes.

One hand gripping the banister, the other titling his wine glass, Nate choked the rest of the desert dry Merlot. He jerked his head back up as he swallowed. Trails of tears sliced out of his eyes, the first tears he cried since the night he became the sole resident.

"Thank fucking God for wine," Nate slurred in short-lived praise as he found both his cup and bottle had runneth empty.

Skitter skitter bom bom bom, came noises from the bedroom window. Nate swung around. Was it raining already? The forecast did not have the deluge scheduled for another couple of hours.

Bom bom MEOW.

Nate parted the curtain sheers nonplussed. "Not now, Mocha," he grumbled.

The neighbor calico pawed and purred on the sill awaiting attention. Her vigorous tail not so subtly swished the empty food dish beside her.

Nate rolled his eyes. "You feed 'em once," he said under his breath. The critter was the finest example of opportunistic scavenging fed into by one person since move-in. Nate opened the window to remove the dish and reminded the cat, "Jamie's not here so go look for treats somewhere else."

Mocha, admittedly skilled at word recognition but lacking other animals' remarkable ability to comprehend disruptions in permanence, perked only at 'treats' and purred excitedly.

"My mistake," Nate conceded, "I said the magic word." He shooed at her with his free wrist, "Please, go away. Tonight's not a good night."

Mocha mewed and bobbed her cheek affectionately along Nate's hand.

Nate was not prepared for such a display and snapped his wrist back. "No, that wasn't an invitation. Please!" He almost shoved the cat to the pavement below.

"MOCHA," a voice called beneath them.

Mocha perked and Nate put his hands where anyone could see them. Hearing the subsequent shutter clicks, though, made him relax. It was just his downstairs neighbor, Max, again. Ducked upside-down out of his own loft and glued to his camera, he promptly arrived to crash and capture, as usual in recent times, the best moment of inopportunity.

"Mocha, there you are—oh, hey Nate, what's up," Max exclaimed. "Hope you don't mind the picture. Can't have enough pics of mates or the fuzz bud in the collection. Inserts some candid joy into the monotony of developing, you know what I mean?"

Nate frowned, "No, I don't know."

Lowering the camera, chill ole' Max shifted gears and his hipster beanie, "How you been doing, anyway? Do you need anything?"

Nate shrugged.

"Ok. Um. Well. Come down one night. When you're free! Remember that 'Inside the Painter's Studio' concept Jamie and I fooled around with? You will really dig the shots I got off of him, some real vibrant stuff. Plus," the kitty cat had rejoined Max for belly rubs and together they threw up so much goofy cheer, "Mocha's up for visits between her joneses for treats."

With a nicety of control, Nate picked up the food dish and cast it down for Max to catch. "Treats do not live here anymore," he said and slammed the window in their faces.

The first thunderclap of the impending storm rocked the sky.

Nate turned and tangled himself up in his own feet. He tripped towards the desk occupying the far wall. The arms of the antique rolling chair broke the stumble but not the smarts of the sprain in his shins. Nate massaged them, facing the desk.

Jamie's studio.

Many nights Nate passed this place by, having emptied it of all except the flecked pigments irreversibly soaked on the desk's surface. This was the heart of the home. Nate would be wherever, Jamie would be here imagining, puffing up at his wispy tufts of hair that Nate would sometimes admittedly sneak up and tussle just to get a rise or a playful shove and hug out of him. Most beautiful of all was the joking never faltered Jamie's creative spirit.

43

Do spirits actually falter? Nate wondered.

He vocalized the ponderance, albeit a bit ramble-y, to the air thick with memories, "Where are you, Jamie? You're not the type to vanish. You were going to paint your masterpiece here. Remember? The landscape portrait of Chicago building over itself throughout history. I was going to throw you a lavish unveiling." Too drunk to decide if he fumbled for it or if it stayed true to possessed form, the box shyly jutted out from underneath the desk and made its way to the top to join Nate. Nate dug under the taped seams and bunched them up. "But you kept wanting to go for more and I—now—"

Nate ripped the Band-Aid off the box. The flaps sprang open. Cardboard dust flew up.

He coughed, evoking more tears. Reaching for the maw, the tears stung as he unpacked the box's contents across the desk. All laid out, it was all so plain:

Jamie's stuffed leather satchel. His watercolor palette. The careworn brushes. Last—

Nate froze as he reached the last. He could tell it was paper, rolled up. He lifted it out and split the rubber band holding it together.

The alcoholic soothes transitioned suddenly to blistering hangover.

The paper unrolled. It was—

...*the l-l-last M-m-moment...*

Nate couldn't bear to look. He catapulted from the desk and jetted to the kitchen downstairs.

Chapter 7

Upstairs, a symphony queued in Jamie's studio.

The poised conductor, an imperceptible, razor thin fissure of space, was the exact size of a musician's guiding wand. The partial players, every tangible molecule hovering about The Loft, were halted to a standstill by a polarized magnetism exposed by the fissure. They treaded in place, awaiting the approaching interlopers for which there are no rational names except maybe 'Stuff of Nonsense.'

Nonsense they may have been, they were as purposeful as they were strange.

Sssss fissss crack!

The nonsense commanded the diminutive slice of time aside with a nearly inaudible spark. Stunned, the surrounding real time observed as packs of shimmering orbs trickled 'cross the fissure. Their trajectory was aimless at first, gathering their bearings as tourists in this world. But as they flitted over Jamie's desk, they synchronized into a ballet to tenderly kiss his personal effects—his palette, his brushes, his satchel—and pollinate luminosity off their silver bellies until time was sure enough to carry on calmly.

Orb to orb, dust to dust, all the matters settled together and the fissure waved its wand and sealed up. The players were ready and the symphony began at the stroke of midnight.

Twelve tinny pulls on a harp sprung the packs of orbs high up towards the ceiling. Then, as quickly as they appeared they disappeared out from one sense: sight.

They evolved to touch. The string section of the orchestra mimicked the flowing pattern of the outside wind and rustled left the pale curtain sheers. Another flow, they rustled right.

A rest.

Hushed, tiptoeing plucks crept out and beckoned all the veiled orbs towards the middle.

The trill, annunciating burst of the violin tuned and called, scuttling aside the bits of time, letting loose the phenomenal trails of energy to snake and *danse* to and fro.

Pillows fluffed as their coziness was tried. The brass twirled up the bed skirt and untied some dress shoes' laces. Percussive mallets struck the paint brushes' limbs. The woodwinds blew the papers, the windows and the lights—so dim! The energy imbued everything, no stone left unturned. Upstairs, The Loft crescendoed, upholding the sacredness, amazingly, of all it discerned.

Meanwhile, back downstairs...

Seven empty wine bottles clinked as Nate wedged an eighth into their recycling crate and thirstily shredded the foil off a ninth. The corkscrew grated down and hollowly popped the cork. Nate flooded his empty glass and in a fell swoop drowned his burgeoning hangover.

Nate moved on to raid the refrigerator. He foraged for any inhabiting leftovers, culling miscellaneous sandwich parts and assorted vegetable sticks. He crammed slices of bread down the toaster's throat. Then, dangling a carrot stick between his lips, he fumbled the cupboard for a less nutritious selection to soak up his overserved liver. A bag of potato chips fatefully flung themselves—

Nate did a double take, he did not touch those.

—to the rescue.

Nate, drunk, gratefully shrugged nonetheless. He cracked off a hearty bit of vegetable and washed it down with a handful of fat laden carb. He clanged a plate to the counter. The toaster ejected his bread.

Crunch, crumble, clink, clang, cloosh. The cacophony pleased Nate's bitter ears and he augmented the hasty dinner plating with the wet peel of processed cheese slices and flatulent, squirtable mustard.

About to round the granite-top island to the living room, Nate caught a whiff of a strange smell. He stopped and sniffed air around the kitchen. It took a moment for him to place the odor.

It was oddly electric, like the faint burning of a short circuit.

Nate swatted to try and dissipate the odor while he scoured each and every outlet, even leering into and unplugging the toaster, just in case. The last thing he needed was The Loft on fire. Completing the search, nothing turned up and the smell had gone on in an instant. Nate shook his head. Taking a farewell swig, he decided to bid the bottom shelf booze goodnight and busied himself with the more filling plate of food en route to the couch.

* * *

The foil chip bag on the counter crinkled inwards. Taken

hold by an invisible hand, it bunched up…and levitated. The flap opened wide. Potato chips floated out and started to casually stroll about the kitchen when several of them suddenly shattered into crumbs. Something was snacking. More chips followed suit, floating and shattering, the addictive cycle of potato chips on loop. The remainder of the bag was completely polished off and whatever did it politely folded and tossed the empty bag into the trash.

* * *

A half-chewed bite of sandwich plopped onto Nate's lap. Robotically, he kept chewing. He was transfixed by the TV where reruns of primetime's spiciest melodrama re-unraveled. Their plots were just as telegraphed and hackneyed as they were last airdate. The male lead, though, was just as shirtless and now in his snug boxer briefs to balance it all out.

Not until the second commercial break did Nate feel his teeth clicking together and catch himself pawing at an empty plate. He noticed the partially masticated morsel. Solely out of bored completion-ism, he retrieved it and finished the job. He dispensed the plate to the coffee table and focused on the beefcake returning from break.

The flavor-of-the-month actor was just delivered the revelatory news that his girlfriend had not only been cheating on him with his best friend, but that she was in on the blackmailing scheme devastating him since the season opener. The girlfriend now laid elegantly nude beneath the comforter, offering to put it all behind them so they can make true love, not war. She never intended this. The main character's ten pack sweated profusely as he made his choice. After a cymbal-clash dramatic cue, he denied her saying he has more integrity or something or other. He donned his dress shirt and zippered his pants back up.

And interest waned.

The passably steamy encounter had arisen Nate's own boxer briefs. He was tempted to reach inside and mentally rewind to the moment when Mr. Actor had unzipped his jeans and stepped into the moonlight to slowly slip them off and, within network television standards, exhibit the sheen of his brilliant torso tan followed by the outline of his meticulously, spectacularly defined buttocks that had just enough bounce to...

Nate gave a couple tugs and huffed. It just did not feel right. Masturbation felt like cheating, even with a fictional character, on Jamie. And Jamie was dead. Gone. Dead. Gone.

"Dead," Nate mumbled, sounding the word out, teaching it to himself. He added variants, "Gone. Dead and gone. Gone and dead."

Nate's hardon receded.

A light stroking ran through his short, brunette hair followed by playful scuffling. Nate stopped mumbling and reached up to brush away the scuffles. He started to straighten his tousled hair when his eyes widened.

He spun around. "Who's there," he queried The Loft?

Creaaak creak warrrr, the rafters answered.

"Damn you, old wood and," looking at his crotch, "you wood." Something had touched him. Had to have! Nate returned to television. "Fuck it, don't get crazy," he told himself.

Out of his peripherals there was an uptick in light. He thought nothing of it. The light ticked up to bright. And poof! The light extinguished.

Nate glanced over his shoulder. The lamp had turned off. Nate tapped the polished nickel base and ticked it to its lowest setting. He had solely picked these out, the pair of pricey touch lamps flanking the couch. He enjoyed their gizmo-y aspect. By the time he and Jamie were moving in, Nate had figured it was now or never to indulge. Tapping the base to up the light the next notch, Nate chuckled. Jamie would tease him so much about these lamps.

"Oh, so NOW you want to be trendy," Jamie's best bitchy queen imitation rang. "The ah-tist's hubby filling his cah-stle with gadgetry."

Nate pictured the wee shove he had given Jamie when he had said that, also recalling the friendly reminder of who was footing the deposit and first months' rent. Jamie had responded by landing a juicy peck on his cheek. Once the landlord had left, he landed something juicier and gracious with Nate pressed depantsed against the front door.

Before any discussions of change. Before resentments or squabbles. Back at the point they both rode on cloud nine.

Nate tapped for bright.

Behind him, the lamp's twin went bright too.

Nate, with his chin moping on the arm of the couch, was still reminiscing.

During painting breaks or when he got home from late shifts at the survival job, Jamie would tease Nate, who would usually be reading or generally decompressing, by stealthily fondling the lamps on and off. Nate always fell for it, befuddled and convinced the sensors were defective or overly finicky. Jamie never failed to giggle at his mischief; at what a funny guy he was. Once the argumentative jousting had begun and there were long stretches of no talking, Jamie eased the tension by staying up to his old tricks. And, eventually, they'd laugh, locking hands.

"Trickster," Nate said and tapped off the lamp.

Its twin copied and went dark.

Instantly aware this time, Nate gasped. He shot straight up and dug into the couch.

Rat tat tat, a rickety window clamored. *Rat tat tat,* went its neighbor. *Rat tat tat tat tat,* all together in unison!

Nate tensed. Inaugural pelts of rain struck outside. Nate teetered to his feet. The heavens unleashed the deluge and the swelling sounds of whooshing water filled The Loft. Nate backpedaled from the living room and flicked off the rest of the lights, keeping a cautious, flicking lookout for lurkers in the dark. Either he was not alone in The Loft or the storm made The Loft too alive. Whichever, it creeped out his already frayed nerves.

Nate scanned the lower level. Satisfied enough by hearing only the rain, Nate mustered the backbone to break away and get the hell to bed to sleep this through. He started up and knocked his shin on the foot of the stairs. He exhaled his pain and tension hard. It condensed and billowed up in a vaporous cloud. Nate saw the breath and felt a cool patch graze his chest. Taking another step, he was shocked; frozen in his tracks as raw chill encircled and ensnared him.

The panicked breaths from Nate's mouth bloomed straight up a vertical shaft of ruptured space. Its icy grasp clutched Nate like a vise. It made him squirm with fright until the growing plumes of his silent struggle surrounded him in an astonishing hue.

Cerulean.

The mystical tint of the cold swirled about the shaft, a self-made sky of ethereal blue.

"What's your favorite color," Nate *awkwardly asked on the first date, so shy.*

Jamie tried not to titter and bit his lip, so attracted. "Guess," he said.

"Green? Like your eyes?"

"No, but I'm glad you like my eyes."

Nate blushed.

"I like yours too and not just because we match," Jamie said chin rested on palm.

Nate raised an eyebrow, emboldened out of his shell, and coyly ventured, "Then, handsome, are you going to make me guess all day or do I have to wait for the second date?"

Jamie flashed his pearly whites.

"You'll have to wait," an otherworldly murmur said atop the stairway.

Nate's muscles and bones jumbled and the shaft vanished, dropping him to his knees.

The presence moaned gutturally. Hesitating not, it whisked all air aside and flew towards Nate.

Nate shivered as his perception became paralyzed. The stairway began to elongate, warping every which way like rubber. Nate anchored himself to the banister but even that boundary felt fake. Acids bubbled up from his stomach and impossibly collided with the firing ions of his brain, mish-mashing nausea and sadness and fear and nostalgia. Everything he wanted to say and was obligated to do fought to be heard, gurgling and screeching, overpowered by the puerile *fucks, shits* and *damns* his defenses raised for his conscience to hide behind.

Velvety caresses sluiced his shoulders. Nate nuzzled the wooden pegs imprisoning him in the stairway. They chafed, scraped, and cut him. He needed to touch something—something tactile—to combat this mystery he was wildly curious about, yet too afraid to solve.

The presence gently squeezed Nate...

...and hugged him.

Weightless tingles buoyed Nate's aching soul. Prevailing cowardice, however, turned a sharp shoulder to the presence and pushed Nate to crawl away, up the stairs. The Loft behaved with more spatial propriety at every step.

The presence attempted to give chase but Nate angrily yelled back, "What are you? What do you want? Are you even real?! If you were you'd help me because—because—" He grappled his way up onto the bed. "—I don't know if I'm capable of helping you." He buried his face in the pillow and pounded his fists. "Please. I need...I need...I need."

Exhaustion melted and fused Nate and the pillow together. The pitter-pattering sheets of rain silhouetted over them as they dizzily tumbled to sleep, spinning around and around and around.

Nate awoke some time later to find that the pillow and the bed were gone.

Chapter 8

Nate hung, prone, suspended in midair like a ragged marionette by what an innate hunch told him were strings. Groggily, he squinted and discerned Nothing: a black maw—cavernous and bottomless. Rain drops fell, scattered, to a floor far, far away. Nate reached down and dangled a hand, testing the distance if a fall were to occur. It was an immediate no brainer: the fall would land instantly...or never. No in between.

This was a threshold. Cross it or die trying.

Dabs of pale watercolor mixed in the rain and stained the abyss.

If this leads to Jamie, so be it, Nate decided. *Cut me loose.*

The strings acquiesced and severed, plunging him down the gargantuan pit.

Neon red scorched the ether.

* * *

EMERGENCY EXIT, the sign blazed over the archway. Nate shuffled out from under it pinching his nostrils, blinded by a residual pain nagging him since...since...

Ugh, time. An irrelevant construct, Nate thought, annoyed and oddly philosophical.

Unable to dispel the irritant, Nate relied on hands and ears to navigate. He deduced by slickness and rock-hard surface that he was walking a concrete pathway. When the trail suddenly gave out and he hobbled to catch himself on a slippery railing, it became clear he was in another stairwell, going down.

Carefully managing the descent, wafts of heat slowly tantalized the nape of his neck. Their vagueness determined them to be of markedly distant origin, for heat rises and loses luster, but not impact if the source is strong. The charged degrees worming their way up his optic nerve clearly emanated from brilliance.

In a blink, Nate's retinas invigorated and he shrieked, peering over the railing at thirty stories of vertigo-inducing stairs. The heat licked his lips and defied gravity to withdrew below. They invited Nate to come along, issuing one disclaimer:

Abandon all hope, all ye who enter here.

Nate's mouth tasted like gravel. His dress shoes clicked monotonously story by story. Sweat amassed in the caves of his armpits and stained his button up. The flights were neverending. The disclaimer rang true.

Sixteen, maybe seventeen flights later, Nate felt he had made progress, was getting close, so he took a break. He rested on the boxy landing bathed in neon red, loosening his tie and undoing the top button of his shirt. Fanning himself, he noticed the heavy metal door framed in the wall. It had a tiny, rounded handle and a frosted glass porthole with dim, white fluorescent lights fizzling behind it. Had one of these been on every landing?

Maybe this is where I get off, Nate surmised.

A hunched shadow whipped past the porthole.

Nate gripped the guard rail.

The shadow darted its hand back and flexed its pincers across the frost. A second, swarthier set of digits swung from the opposite end to clasp the first and wrestled it about. Bulbous heads belonging to each lurched forth, locked in a wrathful challenge of muscle.

The challenger triumphed and both rested. Slowly, aware they were being watched, they turned towards Nate.

Break time was over. Hurriedly, Nate scaled the downward spiral without looking back. Swaths of neon red and alternating *noir* appendages taunted him at every turn until, finally, he reached the bottom where a towering bank of generators hummed, revealing the initial heat's source. A door—the last door—made of steel awaited around the bend. Nate broke for it and hurled himself at the latch—

* * *

—and tripped out into the alley behind work. Early evening's sunset gleamed. Financial bros from adjacent offices haggled over sales figures while swapping pulls on their electronic cigarettes. A duo of their brethren exited from the same fire door Nate had and joined them.

The wrestlers?

Dumbfounded, Nate whined. He craved a bottle of hard liquor with a suicide chaser. There was not much more of this cerebral mushing he could take before quitting time. Powers that be sieved him to this Moment...now the fuck what?

'What' tapped Nate on the shoulder. Jolted, he wound up a punch.

"Whoa! Easy there, slugger," Janelle said, fake dodging Nate as he pivoted at her.

Nate caught up to himself in total shock. "Oh my God, Janelle! I'm—I'm—oh my God," he offered as semblance of apology.

"It's fine! Relax, all's chill." She meant it. "You ok? You look like you've seen a ghost."

The sentiment, not the term, registered with Nate. "I've been having a strange, strange…nothing really, I'm fine actually," he said flouncing in place, self-conscious at how preposterous he sounded and how pale he must be. Janelle's furrowed brow confirmed both so, shifty-eyed, Nate reversed the questioning, "Were you waiting for me? How'd you know I was leaving through the back?"

"It wasn't difficult," she replied, amused. "You told me you were."

"Oh."

Janelle smiled warmly with no intent to pry. "What do you say to taking it easy tonight and coming with me for a good time," she offered instead. "I can sense you need it."

"Easy is the operative word," Nate let slip. The truism made him sag. "Alright, yep, please. Lead the way," he said, stepping aside.

Not one to stand on ceremony, Janelle linked her knit-sweatered arm with his and coaxed him to follow beside her. "My idea of a good time is a little different than other folks," she said. "I hope you don't mind experiencing new things."

Knowing all about new experiences as of late, Nate followed her passively.

Janelle and Nate maneuvered around the private douche-fest

and departed the alley. Wrapping up themselves, the bros filed in the wheezy fire door to run up and retrieve their briefcases before heading to happy hour.

Chapter 9

"This is one of my favorite places," Janelle squealed as they walked in, a delighted kid in the candy store. Nate saw the appeal right away.

The Edge of Broadway Antique Mart spanned half a block near the city's northern lakeshore, comprising itself of interlocking mazes stuffed with expensive kitsch only affordable on impulse. Atomic Age mannequins greeted and advertised along the storefront's shag carpeted gallery. Right now, they were adorned in the last gasps of Fall fashion circa a smorgasbord of eras. If arriving patrons looked close enough, they would notice the dolled-up plastic faces following their every move. Such was the charm of the eclectic shop, succinctly put by the calligraphed notice behind the register:

People perish. Your junk doesn't.

The audacious camp made Nate drop his jaw and go full out limp wristed.

Janelle enunciated her enthusiasm, "Isn't this FAN-TAS-TIC?"

"I'm living for this," Nate belly laughed. Humor surged his veins. Everything looked so bright and cheery and inviting.

Surfing the high, not allowing it to drop, Nate spotted a clothing rack and excitedly pointed. "Um, if that is a leopard print kaftan we HAVE to start there."

Janelle was just waiting for the suggestion. "The world is our fabulous oyster."

Sixties doo-wop grooved from the store speakers and sucked them in.

An absurd pearl broach adorned the garish top, making the ensemble well suited for drag queens and Seventies variety show hosts. Nate sashayed his hips to make the kaftan flair. Janelle pasted on some Coke-bottle sunglasses to complete the outfit. Nate, pouty-lipped, purred and clawed, indeed living for it! The two traipsed the aisles, exchanging trash style for trash style. In the hall of supposedly valuable colored glass objects, they dubiously flipped price tags and stuck their tongues out if the cost was deemed too outrageous. By the end of the hall their tongues were tired. The entire time, from the peculiar Depression-era knick-knacks to the sleek tables of typewriters, Nate was agog and, in a word, joyous.

By reaching the eye of the antique labyrinth, they reached everyone's perennial favorite: the crates of vinyl records. Nate and Janelle flipped through, unearthing personal goodies and surprising novelties.

"Belinda," Janelle exclaimed, admiring a pink-sleeved record like an old friend. "Now there's some pop I haven't listened to since I was a tween."

Nate giggled, reading the liner notes on a Bruce Willis album ludicrously being hocked for seventy bucks. "Tween? Was that even a term when vinyl and MTV ruled the world?"

She smacked him playfully over the head. "When you're my age you'll learn you can retroactively co-opt slang as you damn well see fit."

"Yes, ma'am," he jabbed and beamed at the notes, not really reading them anymore. He was basking in how amazing it felt to sass for a good reason. It felt...fun. "No one's seen me this flaming in a while. Can only imagine my superiors catching me trying on pastel blouses with *Golden Girls* shoulder pads."

Janelle inserted her hand over the sleeve and lowered it. She was also beaming. "You're a real doll, Nate," she said, "I hope you know that. If you don't, I'm telling you. Being the fairly new 'kid' on the block, makes me glad you're my first work friend."

Friend. In four years of being an accounting firm lackey, Nate had never employed that turn of phrase for any of his colleagues. It was just get in, get out and crunch those numbers all about. He would rush home and occasionally met acquaintances at best, seldom...friends.

"You're mine too," he said of the foreignness. He was at a momentary loss for words but suddenly he kept on, liking how nice and easy talking was. "A lot of my college buddies and I lost touch after we moved our separate ways. Several jetted to the East Coast, a few West. Only a handful stayed home. I landed in Chicago, of course, got the first job I wanted—current one—and little by little our texts back and forth were more like 'Hey, what's ups' every few months. And we'd forget to respond. Eventually we never did and they were gone. I figured that was that. Gone is gone, never coming back. Flash forward to now and that's still that. I try to rebuild or create relationships. Sometimes too hard. Regardless, I feel unseen for what I can give a lot, even if it is too much. Maybe that's why I'm left alone. They felt unseen too."

He regained awareness that he was in public and clammed

up, butterflies in his stomach. They had moseyed to the section dedicated to festive décor, the upcoming month's All Hallowed holiday the highlight.

Janelle wiped a tear, smearing her mascara, and brushed aside a curtain of cotton spiderwebs to step in clear view of Nate. "You are a humbler man than you are giving yourself credit for. Anyone should consider themselves lucky to be your friend. Or more. I'm asking myself right now why no one has snatched you up." Nate avoided her gaze for the leering, ceramic jack o' lanterns. "Hey, we barely know each other even as cubicle mates, I understand. Just also understand that whatever's on your mind, you can always bring it to me so it doesn't suck it out of you. That's what the goals of friends are." Nate twirled a pack of rubber bats hanging off the ceiling. Janelle patted his back and busied herself in a mantel ornament spelling out B-O-O. "I hope you don't take that as me harping on you for something I have no idea about. But I meant what I said earlier, you literally looked like you'd seen a ghost."

Nate looked at the ornament as Janelle made her comment. He lifted it from her.

BOO.

Ghost.

What a simplification.

Is what I witnessed in The Loft really that simple? Can I trust her enough to ask?

Nate tabled the ornament and cleared his throat. "May I ask you something private?"

Janelle nodded.

"Do you believe that, maybe, in some way…gone isn't gone?"

"How do you mean? Like, what's gone?"

"Well, like the sign in front says, 'People perish. Your junk

62

doesn't.' Like it lingers around or comes back to you. I guess I'm asking instead of only things perishing and lingering can the same idea apply..."

"To people," Janelle assumed the finish for him.

"Yes," Nate shortly affirmed.

Janelle was sure not prepared for this poser. She searched Nate's expression to check if he was kidding. His humor, though, had turned grave. Grave and serious. She could now see the pain he was in and the fear the question raised. So, out of decent courtesy, in the middle of the antique mart, she mulled it over.

In her time, she had kept many appointments with the grim reaper and the funeral parlor. She could hear the ironically euphoric dirges old Earl played on the pipe organ every time someone went. In her family, when death knocked you answered in your best attire and passed on shining. No one ever said anything about coming back. After paying your respects, you went home to the memorial breakfast and moved on. She accepted this when she was younger. Even had her own frilly dress picked out for when her time came. Then she grew up, matured and remembered thinking, once, about when her estranged, temperamental father passed away and if the dirt was the only place everything about his life was buried in.

This type of contemplation, to Janelle, usually resulted in nothing except wishful thinking. Nate was coming to her for advice, though. She did not want to get his hopes up attempting to explain the unknown but also did not want to leave him without empathizing with sleepless nights, weirdly knowledgeable whispers...chills.

Janelle spoke before she crawled out of her goosebumps. "I believe," she delicately packaged it, "in unfinished business."

"Mmm-hmm," Nate actively listened. A pregnant pause. "And?"

"And what? I don't know what else to offer."

"Unfinished as in…"

"As in…the mysteries of the universe, I don't know! You spring a complicated question, you get sprung a complicated answer. Energies exist in the world. They exist in different forms and it's your choice how to open up to them and how to fix them if they're broken. Just don't expect them to go by any rule book. And…that's the easiest explanation I got." She could tell Nate needed more but the subject had her winded, so she propositioned, "Can we continue shopping? We were having a lot of fun."

Nate gave it a rest. "Sure, totally. Sorry for dragging it out. I appreciate your thoughts."

"Any time," she said happily. "I appreciate the outreach. Maybe at a more optimal point we can revisit. For now, I'm going to go check out the cookware and then, actually, let's head home. Come look with me?"

"I think I want to go browse books or something."

"Awesome, I think books are a few aisles the other way. I'll meet you up front in a few." She rounded a bend of ornate costume jewelry and disappeared.

* * *

Nate retraced their browsing spree and traversed a previously unexplored offshoot to come upon the eponymous 'Book Nook.' The titles lining the shelves had zero rhyme or reason, ranging from dusty Zane Grey Westerns no one read anymore to the latest passed-around-and-tossed shades of eroticism no one could get off to. But interspersed, there were some bona fide literary gems. Nate missed the quaint thrill of curling up with a good book and scrounged up a couple of paperbacks to take back with him to rekindle the interest. It was one of the easier ways to relax.

"I need easy," he muttered and gathered up his finds to meet Janelle and check out.

His ears began to ring. He jostled for earwax, dislodging nothing and stopped as the ringing intensified and everything around him...

Nate's lips quivered. He dropped the books and did not hear them slap the ground. When he said, 'Hello,' there was only the sensation in his throat. A customer walked by wearing tennis shoes without giving off so much as a footstep.

Robbed deaf. Isolation: defined.

Hhhhhhhhhhhaaaaaaaaaaaaaaaaaaaaaaaaaaaaaaaaaaahhhhhhhhhhhh

singed the air. Nate gulped. It was the books. He perused them warily for the one responsible. Rustles and a scrape drew him to the bottom shelf. A black, leather-bound tome jutted out from the other titles. Nate was trepidatious. The volume insisted and titled up its spine. Nate reached for a closer look, touched it, and the ringing faded. First ambient, then total sound returned. Invested and curious, Nate read the fancy, silver lettering vying for his attention:

CROSSING PLANES: A PARANORMAL'S GUIDE TO THE LIFE AFTER DEATH

* * *

"All set," Nate informed the clerk. He laid a stack of books, paperback and hardcover, at the register, hiding their spines.

Leaning there, Janelle watched the clerk ring them up and asked enviously, "You're buying?"

"Yeah, to keep myself occupied," Nate said confidently, reaching for his wallet. "Reading's a productive hobby to get back into."

"Shoot. Well now I can't leave empty-handed." She gave the counter a cursory scan and waved the clerk over. "Pardon me, sir, can you hand over those Elvis salt and pepper shakers? Please and thank you." The clerk obliged, handing her the squat effigies of The King.

"I didn't know you were an Elvis fan," Nate said.

Janelle forked over exact change. "I'm not, they're just tacky. Enjoy your books." She gingerly sheathed them in her purse and marched away. Nate hugged his books like a schoolboy and brought up the rear, imagining how many other sets of celebrity seasoning busts she must have at home.

The image provoked one last laugh.

Chapter 10

*You are a skeptic in picking up this book. I can always feel
one. 'The Other Side,' as it is so popularly coined, intrigues
you but at arm's length. I completely understand! I was
you. I was an unwitting fool underestimating cosmic
possibilities.*

*Until the day I met them. What a strange day it was—I
hesitate to even call it a day, such limitations of minutes
and seconds are meaningless to a dimension fragmented
by much, much more.*

*I had fallen into a midday's rest after entertaining
afternoon tea with some of my most precious confidantes.
We were discussing the tragic death by long-term illness
of one of our circles' sisters, of whom I had known merely
in passing yet nonetheless mourned for being taken far
too soon from our world. In my vulnerable repose, I
consciously ruminated about her; her place now that she
was admonished of her suffering. How that must have
healed and released her from the bondages of pain. Where
did her pain go?*

*Awakening, the answer appeared. A luminous, celestial
projection (that I now understand to be ectoplasm) hovered*

o'er my warm body. Its features danced in wild shapes but its face was undeniably feminine. Her hollow whimpers and mere presentation unnerved me to my core. Yet, I was agog!

"Who are you? Tell me what you need," was all I could say.

She dissipated on the spot.

I later learned the ebbs and flows of her mortal life through subsequent summonings and visitations at the home of her loved ones, who were astonished I knew the apparition and further, identified her. The sister's illness was not cleansed in death, leaving her to wallow in eternity. She sought not to scare, but was forced to haunt, a pitiful situation for which I felt obligated to intervene and help one, the other or none at all to move on.

After this, I found my calling: to serve as liaison to the planes thinly separating us whether it be through spiritually enchanted amulets procured at a Moroccan bazaar, specters rising from thin air or ghoulish tales reserved for the campfire. I entreat you, skeptic, to follow your once hapless guide to the undeniable truth.

My name is Astrid O'Toole and this is <u>CROSSING PLANES</u>: A Paranormal's Guide To The Life After Death.

* * *

Plink
    Plink Plink Plink
      Plink Plink Plink Plink Plink Plink Plink Plink
Plink Plink Plink,

driblets leaked from the kitchen sink faucet downstairs with metallic, xylophonic strikes.

A garden spider *scuttled* up a corner of the bedroom and out a crack in the brick foundation.

Coppery taste <u>lined</u> the mucus of Nate's inner cheek as he subconsciously chewed it.

The radiator pipes warped as they warmed up, racing groans across the ceiling. Their ratcheting CLANK's disquieted Nate away from reading and made his back arch to the point of his head nearly touching his raised toes. He pictured being one of the trapped bubbles of air resisting the crushing tide of steaming water.

CLANK!

His back buckled and cracked. He threw the book down on the bed and face planted in the mattress as the radiator finally got to work.

Nate had been devouring the authoritative, yet tonally condescending English lady's spook manual for hours and successfully heightened all his senses to their peaks. Each sense was now searching for 'signs' or 'omens' or 'premonitions' signaling an active haunting. He could hear, see, taste, feel and smell everything in The Loft to the point of paranoia.

Everything except for a ghost or Jamie.

Nate flipped the book back over and rifled its musty, worn pages. He did admire the block-printed illustrations the author used as historical proof of concept: damning portraits of suicide by noose, heathen skeletons chortling at medieval crusaders, plasma orbs romancing the sleeping. Ms. Astrid O'Toole knew her morbidity. But what could she possibly know to impart upon Nate? Why was she of all books lent to him in the mart?

"Skeptic," her haughty voice teased and flapped the pages to a later chapter.

The uncanny had increasingly become his norm, so Nate took the assertive phenomena in remarkable stride.

Scanning the opening paragraphs of the chapter, it was like being beholden by Revelations.

* * *

CHAPTER 11
SCRYING

Retiring to her chambers after an evening of requisite domesticity and frivolity, the young lady slips into her gown, sits before the vanity and takes up the brush to straighten her flowing locks of hair before bed. She pauses to gaze at herself. She ponders her beauty, her presence. She sets down the brush to light a candle afire. It is the candle of her wants, and it dimly illuminates her hopeful face.

Deeply gazing upon the reflective glass, the fair maiden concentrates. She returns to the brush and clutches it to her bosom, pairing her being with destiny. In the mirror will appear to her either the grim familiar of spinsterdom or the brilliant vison of the noble suitor who will claim her heart forever.

Scrying—or divination—is an ancient practice not solely reserved for Victorian girls or Hallowe'en parlor games. It is an art of prediction, of finding and of mining the very depths of the personal soul. It is a trance-like act in which one transports the subconscious to summon pieces of the past, present or future via an object, such as a mirror, a crystal ball or vessel of liquid.

To scry requires connection and is easy for any novice to attempt under the correct circumstances and only the most honest of intents.

* * *

Use me, the lighter urged as Nate's thumb fumbled the ignition, reticent.

The personal effects were dispersed across the desktop, prepared to catch the impending candlelight. Ms. O'Toole's instructions—no longer a mere <u>Guide</u>—dictated that ritual props were essential to lend as much essence to the proceedings as possible.

"*The Lantern [that] guides the wayward vision from the edge of one world to the cusp of our own*"

was a chubby candle stub fixed to a dollar store candelabra left over from a party. Nate dug Jamie's oval makeup mirror used primarily for self-portrait modeling out of the closet to frame

"*the art of the scry.*"

Altogether, the setup resembled a tarot reading tent at the carnival but the 'maiden' persisted and bore the superfluous measures, aching to see his suitor.

Nate flicked the lighter. Sparks excitedly spit, wielding a bluish-orange flame that hungrily engulfed the braided wick.

71

The candle sputtered, crackling, rising up by inches to glow the divining shrine. Nate pocketed the lighter and scooted closer. He wiped the dust collected in storage off the mirror with his sleeve so he could clearly stare at his own reflection. This reflection was normally retch-worthy but Nate restrained self-loathing to shift his stare into a gaze. To gaze past himself.

> *"To gaze into the silver eddy of the dreams and desires you never imagined were being had for you, awaiting you beyond the veil..."*

The Loft sounded off as one, this time to draw him in, not distract him away.

Plink
   Plink Plink Plink
    Plink Plink Plink Plink Plink Plink Plink Plink
    Plink Plink Plink Plink,
                    CLANK! CLANK! CLANK!
                            scuttle scuttle scuttle scuttle scuttle
Nibbled-up cheek blood smeared his chops as he licked them.

Spots appeared. Purplish, bruise-like spots. Nate tried to connect them when the mirror began to squeak on its axis. The candle flame surged. Formal configuration of the spots seemed, for sure, imminent!

The mirror squealed and flopped, its screws loose on the sides. Nate blinked in surprise and watched the spots betray themselves as dizzy illusions in his corneas.

"What the Hell," Nate groaned, snatching up the Guide. Everything was set accordingly, nothing could be missing.

"The key is not to rush. Neither anxiety nor rash impatience have places in the act of divining as they lead to undesirable results. Relax. Sever yourself from outside stressors prior to scrying. Tether to your entity and the force will be indelible."

Nate cast the lecturing book to the floor. It coasted into the banister, flapping open to another important, predestined chapter stop. Nate bluntly ignored it, grappling instead to tighten and reposition the mirror.

"I'm not stressed. I'm not stressed," he chanted. He decided how to dub himself. "I'm exploratory," he decided as the last twists fixed the screws. Huffing, he gazed again with more longing. "Jamie," he pled, "if you're really in there or out here or anywhere, please show me. You're not resting. Nor am I. We really should settle the matter."

Nate paused and glanced at the effects almost humorously. "Mmm, this'll make you come out," he said secretively. He picked up one of the paint brushes and rubbed it in one of the watercolor pans: goldenrod, the sublime hue of sunrises, sunsets and treasure. Nate twirled the brush between his fingers then ran it across the mirror, leaving behind jaundiced strokes of the dry pigment. Jamie would get that *adorably perturbed* face when Nate fooled around with his brushes and paints.

You're squandering my valuable, irreplaceable supplies, Jamie would allege.

Nate turned the brush on himself and tickled his usual punishment on the tip of his nose. He wistfully clutched the brush to his heart, feeling it enlarge two sizes in a beat.

"Come punish me some more, love," he said. "Please punish

me.

The burden of the body floated away.

His gaze leveled.

Scrying, he mouthed, "Help me."

The book pages quivered by the banister.

> *"The corridors of the netherworld are treacherous. They are long, twisting chutes; a gauntlet spirits are forced to navigate in order to roam free into the land of the living. Perils await around every corner. Ghosts, same as their mortal counterparts, contain dichotomies of the soul that are easily split by the intense planes that make up the spiritual cosmos. These dualities—classically known as good and evil—can become enemies and, worse, predators. I testify to both ends of the spectral amicability spectrum. It is in my expert opinion to implore you, dear skeptic, to fathom that scrying is not a substitute for rational thought. It is a delicacy and must be treated as such. Do not scry for long. What you do not understand about the Unknown, it already does about you with the ability for more as I will soon explain if it suits you to take heed."*

Nate's reflection was wiped clean away. A murky pool of residue stealthily rippled behind the mirror glass. The candle plunged into it. Stick and flame alike splashed, the flame growing hotter. Two glints shot out of the wake and swam a distance to lodge themselves equidistant from one another center-mirror. The granules of goldenrod flared a halo around the oval frame. Like a gaping womb, the residue churned into labor. Gummy, amorphous features started to fitfully protrude the elastic barricade. Poufy blond bangs prevailed followed by soft lips, and a tweakable nose. The glints burned viridian. As they aligned with the emerging distinctions they blinked open, twinkling hazel.

Nate was awestruck. "I don't believe it...Jamie?!"

The birthed vision's acknowledgment was enigmatic and curt.

The urge to dance around the room knocked Nate's knees together but kept still to avoid breaking the miraculous scry. He hunted for words. This was Jamie, his long-term boyfriend, it should not be difficult to find something to say to him!

Nate felt a tad stupid as he only managed to utter, "Um, hi." Then, "Can you talk?"

Smartass eyebrow raises told him of course not.

"Duh," Nate slapped his forehead and laughed. "Common sense, right? I had to ask. God, there's so much more to say than just 'How you doing.' I just...oh, Jamie. You don't know how much I needed—need you. I need you so badly. These past months..." He ventured his hand towards the mirror. If talk was not an option, perhaps...

The vision regarded the gesture curiously, figuring it, and bobbed a cheek to approximate the contours of Nate's hand. Judging the intimacy, the vision mimed an additional nuzzle and soft, lids-closed ecstasy.

Nate traced the sensational transferal along his lips. "I almost forgot what you were like," he said, aroused. Forever. He needed this for forever. "Wouldn't forever be splendid, dear," his arousal vocalized.

The vision rocked in place and cast a furtive glance over its shoulder. It rushed a flirty smile and puckered up.

To kiss. Nate paused, sensing the finality of the action. Just like the end of the Moment; that old dream. "Wait a minute," he said.

Too late. The vision blew a peck as the reflection of the candle splashed back to the forefront. The candle had reached wick's end and, without warning, extinguished the vision, leaving behind only smoke and mirror.

"NO," Nate cried, spewing rapid 'noes' as he yanked open drawers in search of another candle. "Come on, come on, come on, there has to be—" In the back of a bottom drawer there was. Nate broke off the finished candle and speared the next onto the candelabra. "Come back, come back, come back," he beseeched, scraping the ignition.

A new flame sputtered and Nate gazed to find his scry was receding, but not gone.

"Thank God, I thought I lost you," he said. The vision's sentience was already different and stronger; frowning at him. It shifted side-to-side glances behind and around it, beleaguered by a restlessness. Like it was being followed. Returning Nate's gaze, its frown was not just sad, but feeble. "Jamie, what's the matter," Nate's quaveringly questioned.

The vision blinked, hazel blazed back to viridian and began to fade themselves with the rest of its features.

"Jamie, no, stay!" The halo of goldenrod vanquished. Nate retaliated sternly, "Why are you always leaving?!" The vision gave pause. "If you really wanted to help us, you would stay."

Jaded bitterness crossed both sides of the mirror.

"We—and I—left things as we shouldn't have. This is our chance to make it right. To start over. Isn't that why you 'visited' in the first place? That's why we're here now."

Threads of hazel softened in and once more unto the breach, the vision approached to listen.

Nate badly wanted to cup its hands, if it had hands, as he spoke, "We have so much to talk about. Let's catch up. I'll start with me."

He ignored the second eyebrow raise that seemed to say *as usual.*

"I've been keeping up with therapy like we decided. Seeing the same person, Linc. Ok, I admittedly have slipped off a few weeks but only because I am trying to figure things out for myself. For us. Work is...paying the rent. Feels like sleepwalking. Sleep-working. I'm not always sure what I do there anymore. There are a lot of opportunities." Even if the talk was about him, an easing aura pricked Nate's skin and made him sigh. "Oh, that must be you too. You're everywhere around me, Jamie. I have tried so many ways to make sense of my life. Gazing at you now, I know I've been brought to the right place. To the solution."

The vision cocked its head low, exhibiting signs of concern.

"Never in a million years would I have believed anyone trying to convince me a ghost was real. But they are real! You are real! This mirror trick is the missing link: you. Your body."

The vision motioned to argue.

"Now I know what you're going to say," Nate cut the vision off, "this is impossible. Jamie, no. We can do this. We can scry every night. I'll come home, you'll be in the mirror waiting for a call. We can talk and joke and move back in together. The *ah-tist* and his lover!" With witless conviction he resolved, "We can find the way to have it all like we always wanted."

The vision froze up as a concealed fright snuck up and poked it from behind.

Nate happily clapped his hands, mistaking the gaping for excitement.

"Oh my God, this is so wonderful," he yelped. "We should toast. Or, I will and we'll continue picking up right where we left off." As Nate slid back his chair, he remembered a teensy, finite, little detail. "Wait, I can't look away from you." He chewed his lip. "You seem to have summoned enough strength to stick around this long." The request following came out as if he were addressing an infant or a child, "Promise me you will not disappear when I go downstairs. I will be gone less than a minute. Do you promise?"

There was no way of knowing for sure. Nate acted on trust and stood up, tiptoeing backwards towards the stairs. The vision did not falter in the candle's glow. Craning his head away a fleeting second to see where he was going, Nate twisted back around and, lo and behold, the vision sustained itself. Smiling, Nate's heel kicked the Guide offering the new chapter. Nate sidestepped it and skipped down the stairs.

"Look at who is leaving who now," Astrid O'Toole gibed.

"Back off, bitch, I'm not doing anything wrong," Nate said, halfway downstairs.

Squealing rubber and the coarse whines of metal on metal suddenly screeched the air and grated the membranes of Nate's inner ear canal. All lights in The Loft blinked. Nate nearly tripped his way to a broken neck and shouted useless obscenities. What was that? It sounded almost like a car...

Nate gasped. *Car.*

CRASH! Wood met wood. Glass shattered.

Nate's spine twisted and stretched to try and see over the bedroom landing, hoping it was not what he feared. Stomping back up...

...the mirror was toppled face down in a wake of its own glass shards. Whimpering, Nate hurled himself at the desk. He set the mirror upright and clumsily tried to piece the empty, plain shards together with his bare hands.

A blustery force whooshed behind him. All the windows were closed and outside it was no longer windy. Nate held a triangular, inches-long shard in his right hand as he noticed the force.

It felt unlike any other: Larger. Firmer. Warmer.

THUMP.

Weighty steps approached like heartbeats both on the floor...and the ceiling.

Thump.

His legs jellied.

Nate looked at the broken mirror. His throat closed. Deep splintery scratches marred both sides of the frame. A way had been definitely found and...clawed out.

Could it be?

Hhhhhhhhhhaaaaaaaaaaaaaaaaaaaaaaaaaaaaaaaaahhhhhhhhhhh

repeated the same, singeing tone as the book shelves prior in one continuous, grisly moan when, from above, a blunt punch to Nate's skull plowed him down to his right. His arm broke the fall and slipped his palm along the slender shard. Rolling over, Nate dropped the glass and saw the lines of crimson gore coursing out from the sliced flesh.

In a dizzy spiral he fainted on the spot with a dull thud.

* * *

Nate's right hand twiddled in and out of focus as he came to the next morning. The shape of the hand was real. The whorls of the fingerprints were real. The hard encasements of the nails were real. Alas, Nate did not believe the hand as a whole was real.

A hairline scratch ran up the center. Nate prodded it with his left and felt a tiny sting. Nothing bled out. It did not even appear to require any stitching or bandaging whatsoever. Nate woozily pushed himself up and noticed the criminal shard of glass beside him: clear and clean.

Where did I fall now? he questioned the bright dawn engulfing The Loft. One of the windows rattled. Nate furtively glanced at it out of the corner of his eye and spied something else sway. Something translucent.

The curtain sheers.

He rolled over, avoiding pressure on the scarred hand. Aside from the wound, he had almost zero recollection of the night before. He could tell, however, that whatever happened, the windows were never, ever open to let in a breeze.

Nate teetered to his feet, using the desk for support. The fractured mirror and watercolor supplies were still spread out in a shrine. Regarding them, though, Nate felt no attachment. The objects were devoid of meaning; of physicality. They were just...purposeless things.

Hushed talking, weird gibberish, and another window rattle bought his attention.

He inched closer.

The curtain sheer billowed out and elegantly flowed in and around the frame of an invisible man. Telling signs of a face protruded and, from there, Nate imagined the man was roughly five-foot-six or -seven. The bottom of the sheer bunched about the slender region of where calves ended and ankles began, leading to feet firmly planted on the floor.

Rather than brimming with doubt or fleeing in terror, Nate flushed, oddly, with school boy shyness. Only one idea sat on the tip of his tongue. "Jamie? Honey, is that you," he asked the manifestation. He waved his right hand. "I thought I cut myself on a piece of glass last night. Did you tend to it somehow?"

The manifestation was silent behind the swaying sheers.

Nate stood before the illogical searching for the next logical step. The shyness within made him offer the healed hand to the manifestation. "This feels like a first meetup where you have to shake hands and introduce yourself. Both of you are super lost and, um...I'm Nate."

A grip took ahold, shook his hand and yanked it forward. Nate yelped. New driblets of blood had wriggled out of the wound. The grip held onto Nate tight. He was about to pull away when the grip kneaded his hand tenderly. The blood clumped into a bubble and slid the path of his wrinkled life lines to an unseen mouth where it dispersed into a mist.

"H-h-h-holy sh-sh-shit," Nate sputtered.

The grip released and the manifestation nudged the curtain aside.

Nate almost fainted again. "What are those?"

Stringy jellyfish-like tentacles hovered and crawled in the guts of the invisible man. The blood mist pollinated them, branching them off into baby veins of a 'human' body.

Nate stumbled away.

The invisible man bounded over the bed and did not touch the ground until landing on the desk. The objects of the shrine were suddenly tossed up. The palette was dragged and lifted, one of the pigments—cerulean—depressing in its pan.

Nate sensed agitation. "Jamie, what's wrong? Are you mad? I'm sorry about my reaction if you are." He watched the invisible man rifle the things. "Have you forgotten this place? This is your home. Your things. Do you need me to remind you?"

He stopped. The writing, crude and misspelled, was painted on the wall:

I need u

Nate groaned and curled a passionate smile. How he longed to have such sentiment reciprocated. Attachments to this lone object of his desires resurrected in his groin. "Oh baby," he swooned, "name what you really need, mister, and you got it."

Manically, the manifestation completed its request with a more precise, second verse:

I need u
to Make me LIVE

IV

The Other Side

Chapter 11

The stark no man's land between where the corn rows ended and patches of the concrete jungle began soared by for miles and miles. Maggie scratched at her poufy blond hair tied up in a ponytail. The sight of the prickly prairie grass made her scalp itch. In her rush to catch the passenger train that morning, she forgot to condition in the shower. Settling back in her roomy blue, economy class seat, she knew full well the hotel would have conditioner. She had forgotten a lot in the hustle routine- and packing-wise. Mission-wise, though, she was ripe with mindfulness.

Depleted as the fields were at the moment, Maggie still wondered why Jamie had moved away from all this. He would always pine to her about living in 'the sticks' and how one day he would paint his ticket out of the little Illinois town that offered him no prospects. Maggie never really got it. In agriculture, you always started with nothing. If you wanted anything you tilled the soil, planted the seed and cultivated before the harvest. That was (and is) the bountiful circle of life and that is exactly how Maggie contentedly stayed and lived hers out.

A blot in the distance made her jump. Looking past the smudgy window she thought it was a boy sitting in the grass; a holey-tee-shirted teenager hunching over a—

Maggie returned to her seat and reclined back. In youth, she usually found Jamie drawing in the yard when he should have been helping with the chores. She never tattled about it to Mom and Dad because that is not what good big sisters do. That way too, she realized now, on the train, he would always be in the—or a—yard whenever, wherever. Maggie and, finally, after a few tiffs about tradition and realism, both their parents learned that Jamie simply loved a larger, more unlimited type of culture. The yard was his first launch pad towards a wide-open world for his painterly mind to harvest. He did not hate 'the sticks.' He just hated being held back.

The train crossed past the shiny spires of Chicago's city limits and triggered an ulcer irritating Maggie's stomach.

Where was Nate from again? she found herself asking. She could not recall. He was a small-town boy as well. *What good that taught the bastard. He gets to hide in the city and...*

Maggie blew out some hot air to ease the pain. Where Nate grew up was irrelevant. She was going to root him out however possible.

As the train pulled into Union Station, Maggie gathered her purse and overnight duffel and disembarked. Winding around groups of visiting football fans and Amish folk, she pulled a crumpled business card from her pocket and translated the worn printing into a viable address.

A conductor oversaw the travelers entering the terminal. Maggie tapped him on the shoulder and showed him the card to inquire if her directional memory was serving her well since the last time she visited. The conductor nodded, weaving his hand into a map. She waved some Midwestern good cheer, then glowered as she revolved out the exit to downtown.

* * *

Both the executive's assistant, Valerie, and general office receptionist, Suzanne, hoped that the duffel-toting woman marching out the elevator had gotten off on the wrong floor. The woman's stern disposition appeared normal enough for the business district but there was some real tacit fuming in the way she paused and wildly swung her ponytail to scope out the dual office inlets. Fortunately for Suzanne, one of the accounting colleagues, Janelle, came out in the nick of time to chat about some papers.

Thus, Maggie stepped up and set her duffel on Valerie's desk.

Valerie greeted with a smile. Perhaps this was one of the executive's jilted 'wives' she had not met. Operating on this hunch, her voice over compensated and chirped, "Good afternoon! Welcome to Strotman Incorporated. How may I assist you?"

"Yeah, you can help me find someone," Maggie said.

"Oh! Do you have an appointment?"

"No, I'm—" Maggie cleared her throat, blowing out some more hot air. "Good afternoon, sorry, I haven't had much sleep." Valerie was relieved by the pleasant switch. Maggie continued, "My name's Maggie. I'm here to visit Nate Bowman, I'm a—a—relative."

Valerie clicked open her directory, "Absolutely. Welcome to Chicago! I can look up his extension and give him a ring. Do you know his department?"

Maggie made to verify the business card. "Accounts something or other? Here, I can check."

Overhearing, Janelle intervened, "Excuse me, miss, you said you're looking for Nate?"

Maggie turned, "Hi, yes I am. Is he here?"

"Unfortunately, no. He's been out sick for the past few days."

"Oh." Maggie's head sunk. This mission was going to have to stretch even longer. She snatched her duffel. "Thank you anyway."

Janelle felt bad for the stranger who came all this way, "I can leave a message for you!"

Maggie shook her throbbing head and boarded the elevator. "No. I'll get him later."

Chapter 12

Mocha purred like a motor car. The rhythmic kneads behind her ears were her easy existence's greatest pleasures. Until they were over. The fingers at work collapsed atop her. She peeked over to see that her 'Human Number One' Max had lapsed asleep after a solid hour of heavy petting. She waited patiently to see if he would awaken and realize the error of his ways but no such luck. He was out cold.

Ever the nocturnal night owl, Mocha slinked off the couch and around the various tripods and lampstands peppering the human's photo loft to get to the most important room: the kitchen. The moist kibble mix was emptied into her gullet earlier. The recently regifted treat bowl remained similarly vacant. The spoiled calico mewed her dissatisfaction. No attention coupled with no treats was by no means acceptable.

Sauntering to the front window Max left cracked for her, Mocha leapt and shimmied under her kitty hatch to go for a midnight prowl. By this hour she had free reign of the sidewalks to patrol, everyone and everything except errant insects in appropriate repose. The waxing moon, near full, lit her path better than the scrappy city lamps stationed at sporadic intervals. She rubbed along their bases, however, for they made fantastic scratching posts.

Commotion arose in the back alley. Mocha's ears flipped to listen in as she wound around the light poles, purring. It was just some mild scuffles when the sudden rattles of falling aluminum cans arose her into suspicion. She crouched. One of the cans clinked as something kicked it. Then another. Mocha skulked ahead, wary. No one messed with her turf.

She rounded the corner. The cans laid scattered, ejected from a nearby dumpster. Mocha sniffed the perimeter. The perpetrator had fled. She padded through the scene, all presented clues determining the case closed.

Too soon. Mocha's sonar detected activity in the ivy overgrowth covering the abutting property's chain link fence. It rustled the leaves in every direction, revealing a wall of lascivious pupils ogling her. Without warning, a mischief of mangy city rats, ten or so, scampered and fanned out to surround her, emitting raspy hisses through their sneering buck teeth. They whipped and thrashed their inches-long tails against the asphalt.

Mocha hissed back defensively. Her fur stood on end. She unlatched her claws.

The rats tittered and taunted her with fake attack lunges, their filthy coats lashing wet sewer grime as they did. Mocha fiercely remained steady, retaliation yet a foolhardy choice.

High registering whines streaked out of the sky and raised the rats to their hind legs. They were driven into a rabid euphoria. They pawed worshipfully, hailing psychotic praise as zealots would to a deity; a deity who appealed only to the basest orders. The grizzled leader of the rat pack made itself known by stretching dominantly higher than the rest, leering impishly at Mocha, possessed by a message of ill will from on high. The latter merely sat on her haunches and glared. The head rat clucked, impressed by the disregard, and signaled for withdrawal. The swarm came down from their lunacy and obeyed, scurrying off to pose menace elsewhere.

Mocha calmly watched the pesky bastards depart. Assured they were gone, she peered up to see what in the stars had provoked this most unusual invasion. She found it concealed amid the moonlight: an alien wavelength radiating like a heat source from somewhere close. Following it over, memorable treat hankerings growled in her gut and reminded her of...

Human Number Two!

Mocha gracefully scaled the pathway of pipes and ledges she had mentally forged for herself up to The second floor Loft's bedroom window. She nosed the sill optimistically for snack kibbles. Thwarted again. Human Number Two has been gone a while, she noticed. He was reliably near to open the window and, besides snacks, donate belly rubs gentler than Human Number One's. Human Number Two talked to her too. The words meant little to Mocha but his sweetness and whimsical tone towards the words pleased the feline. After all would be said and done, Mocha would notice Human Number Two staring off like he yearned to follow her outside and join in on an escapade far away from The Loft.

Now, there was just Human Number Three and he did not like her. Everyone liked her. For him, though, her visits seemingly came off as upsetting. So strange, so sad. Perhaps there was a different root cause she did not know about. Moving forward, either way, she would just have to try being extra adorable.

Mocha adjusted her exterior night vision to peer into the dim interior of The Loft.

Figures writhed in the dark.

Human Number Three was unclothed, on his back. His chest was heaving, his arms outstretched, hands ahold of the much less perceptible figure on top who was at his groin. Human Number Three's face was contorting irregularly. Mocha's caring instincts jumped her to the conclusion Human Number Three was in great pain until she watched him bite his lip and hurl both his arms backward. The actions were so primal. Checking out the figure straddling him, Mocha saw, through the figure, a stiff, erect organ being pumped. By the universal comprehension of carnal knowledge, she understood what Human Number Three was feeling was not pain.

Mocha stood guard. She listened as Human Number Three's pleasured moans and dirty talk grew in fervor. She heard him aim a cry directly at the figure. A name. Human Number Two's name! Two had come back! Excited, Mocha was about to bat the window pane to gain both their attention when she saw through her aloofness that...she was seeing through the figure too!

Her fur puffed from the tip of her tail to the tip of her ears. The figure had Human Number Three pinned from the waist down, its weight evident on his stationary legs. Yet, as Number Three climactically began to thrust his hips, the bodily display was fully visible through the radiating wavelength identical to what Mocha had observed in the moonlight.

The wavelength of vermin.

Where Three's organ was being pumped, a bundle of veiny fibers bunched under the figure's hazy epidermis into a makeshift mouth. Similar clumps were spreading to what passed for arms, then hands and out to pointy fingers as the figure mutually started to climax, etching darkened, liquid lines down Human Number Three's inner thighs that were noticeably congruent to the scars of others. The lines bled as the figure's mouth and fingers swapped places. It sucked and swallowed the blood trickling out, fingers pumping furiously. Number Three yelled. His stomach caved and he exploded onto himself. The figure slurped the thigh lines clean and lifted itself from Human Number Three, who was smiling in bliss. Zombie-like, Number Three rolled off the bed and lumbered out of the bedroom to tidy up.

Mocha shook away being stunned and protracted her claws. That was not Human Number Two doing those things in there. That was Human Number Nothing that needed to know who was boss. She scratched at the glass. The figure, several shades bolder, snapped to look without eyes at her in surprise. Its veins wrapped around the burgeoning sinews of muscular legs and the figure sprang out of sight. Mocha bristled, taken aback by its speed.

The window flew open. Mocha leaned in to peek over the sill. The figure descended from above and assaulted its veiny forms at Mocha's fragile neck. Mocha yowled and clawed her attacker. Her hits, though strong, bounced ineffectively off what was not flesh. The figure released one strangling hand and maliciously swiped back. Mocha felt a patch of her side burn. The figure's veins coiled around the region of its mouth and thirstily leaned for the fresh blood, rumbles and gibberish toppling off its forming tongue.

Mocha hissed and maneuvered onto her good side. She shot her claws at the mouth and lodged them inside. Yanking, she clipped a gnarled bramble of them in half. The figure recoiled and released its chokehold. Mocha escaped the sill and haphazardly bounced ledge to ledge, pipe to pipe until she reached her kitty hatch and slid into home. Wincing and terrified, she stashed herself in the nearest open cabinet.

"Mocha, sweetie pie, what's the matter," Human Number One called after her, the flurried entrance waking him. She trembled, licking her wound until it stung too much to continue. Human Number One fell in front of her worriedly. "Oh my God, Mocha," he shouted, gawking. "Mocha! Your side is gashed open! Oh, Jesus, we have to get you to a vet. Who did this to you? Who?!"

She mewed, seeping strength, like a stray kitten losing the hope of ever being rescued.

Chapter 13

Maggie boiled and stewed as she awoke in the hotel room the next morning.

Give him the benefit of the doubt, she had counseled herself. *Give him time to sort things out on his own. Give him the chance to prove he is not a complete son of a bitch.*

The opportunities for clemency passed well over a month and a half ago. The time had come to take advantage of there being no statute of limitations for holding a person accountable and by late afternoon, Maggie was shooting daggers at the entire far-West Loop as she stepped out the 'El' station and began the blocks-long trek to The Loft.

It was not fair that she had to be making this trip at all. It was not about the distance. She was always fine with travelling before. It was that she had given up three unpaid days of work for this. Four if she counted her personal call off.

He ought to pay for all of them too.

Further difficult was that Nate not even have the decency to be easily located. She had to come hunt him in this place.

The neighborhood was not ugly per se. It was just clashing of personas; an inbetweener purgatory of multiple directions wishing to be taken. In the distance were the monumental growths of skyscrapers downtown. Their roots, elder limestones and mid-level brownstones, grew outward for miles at a stretch. Then, there was a lone factory Maggie passed by that was simply clinging on. The parking lot was deserted save for a few ramblers not necessarily there for work. Random developments occupied other shells peppered about. The remaining patches were flat and leveled.

In this Jamie and Nate chose to live: a place of detached, confused disconnect where Maggie was being made to wait.

She leaned against a lamppost across the street from The Loft. It was near the end of the working day. Sooner or later, Nate would eventually have to come home or flip a light on to blow his cover. Then she would demand answers; confront him with the facts she was lugging in her purse. If she did not smack him with them first.

Uncountable increments of joyless minutes were all that passed the corner.

Later, yawning but with all the time in the world, Maggie glimpsed a vagabond bumming toward her across the parking lot wasteland. His tattered hoodie ballooned over his lanky bod, saved from flying off like a kite by the stuffed brown paper bag he carried. Maggie slid her purse closer and side-eyed him to try and catch his face, obstructed by his pesky hood. She disengaged deciding to mind her own business. Curious, though, she could not help but wonder. He was tall, wiry AND headed the right direction.

A fortuitous wind fluttered the hood just enough.

"Nate," she gasped, walking after him, "Nate. NATE! STOP!" He had to be playing dumb. "Nate, I know that's you and I know you can hear me."

It was like she had paused a robot. Nate turned, limbs slow and deliberate, and gaped at her vacantly.

Maggie awaited him to greet her or basically recognize her presence. "I guess you don't remember me," she prompted, pissed. "I'm the recipient of your unwanted mail. Sender of your unanswered text messages and missed calls. Your dead boyfriend's sister."

"Oh, hi Maggie," Nate said numbly.

"Oh, hi Maggie," she mocked. "How insultingly droll of you to say. I came all this way and you can only say 'hi.' After all the shit you pulled? How about how are you? How about what can I do for you? How about sorry? How about let's talk about Jamie? Not just hi Maggie I don't give a flipping, flying fuck about anything or anyone."

"I'm sorry you came all this way," Nate responded.

Maggie's upper lip twitched and she burst into tears. "You're unbelievable." She brushed snot and saltwater on her sleeve. "My parents," she sniffed, "want to maul you. Literally rip you apart. You've met my dad, he's strong and he's got farm equipment." Nate was unfazed by the threat. Maggie pressed her hands together to reason, "Our family, I pray you can imagine, has been in incredible pain. But I have stood up for you, Nate, to the family for longer than I really should have because I knew you and I knew your amazingly dedicated partnership. You two had so, so much. You were each other's first long terms! I acknowledge that you are in huge pain too. But it's entirely pointless for any of us to continue being against each other after all we've gone through and had—the good times! Let's talk."

She was practically speaking to stone. Nate was solid as a filthy block of ice. Nonetheless, Maggie stuck with being even keeled. "Is any of this agreeable to you?"

The wind slipped the hood off Nate's head and Maggie drew

back, aghast. Nate's appearance was abnormally pallid, marred by sallow crow's feet and sunken cheeks. Looking unhealthy was putting it mildly. He looked drained.

"I agree," Nate said gravelly, "there is no reason to be against each other." Maggie let out a relieved sob. "In fact," he continued, "there is no reason to be for each other either."

Maggie watched her hopes rise and dash to the pavement. "Hold up, what?"

"What we had together is changed and done and your involvement is no longer necessary. If you had not pushed and nagged Jamie during your visits to submit all those applications and portfolios we would not have entered this predicament."

Maggie wound her purse up for a whack.

Nate was reminded of the paper sack in his grasp and turned on Maggie indifferently. "Please, excuse me," he dismissed her with, "I have needs to tend to."

Maggie could not believe how flabbergasting this continued to become. She pulled the thick manila envelope, the final straw she had been carrying, from her purse and gave chase. No more pleasantries. This was war. She lashed at him, "So is that what you've been harboring this whole time? That I encouraged Jamie, who I had known far longer than you—aka since he was born—to pursue his dreams? Do you hear how horribly fucking selfish that sounds? I didn't like him going so far away for so long either but you didn't see me being so insecure about it or stressing him out by forcing him to stay. You know he stayed so long because he cared about you? He never stopped raving about Nate. Yet despite having that, you just couldn't let him go for a second because you couldn't be alone."

They had reached the foyer of Nate's building. Nate reached

to stick his key in the security door. Maggie inserted herself to block him, insisting, "Ohhh no, you sure as Hell are not being let off the hook, buddy."

Nate blithely re-attempted his key. "Do not deter me. I have needs to tend to."

"Fuck your needs, Nate." She brandished the envelope and waved it about his face. "I'm serving you ownership. Read this. This is the accident report you mailed me. And here!" She shook her purse and emptied out more papers. She named them, "His obituary. His memorial card. Pictures of him when he was a child. I think you may have been too busy to look at any of it. Just as you were busy when Jamie was in the city morgue and my parents had to go it alone identifying him. Busy when I kept trying to reach out to you when you couldn't do the same. And when we were at the funeral you—you—you know what, screw it." She grabbed for Nate's keys. "I'm actually just going to go up and collect anything else you have of his because if you are not going to honor the memory of my kid brother then you don't deserve to even be around his stuff."

"Don't you fucking touch anything!" Nate dropped the paper sack and aggressively swiped at Maggie's confrontational sheaves and sent them flying as he smacked Maggie back.

Maggie fended off a second blow by shoving his arm and backing away. "Touch me again and I'll have your ass thrown in jail," she warned. Her thumb stung. Examining it, there was a paper gash oozing. She applied pressure, unknowingly dribbling onto Jamie's obituary.

The blood hooked Nate. Transfixed, he bent over to pick up the soiled notice.

Maggie noticed sadly. Before she could apologize to Jamie about bleeding on his memory, she saw the contents of the brown bag beside Nate. Inside was a host of medical supplies: gauze wrap, plastic tubing and scores of disposable syringes. In the process of resisting, she had rolled back one of his hoodie's sleeves. Bruised pockmarks trailed up Nate's forearm.

"Jesus Christ," she said, backing away further.

Nate lustily held up the obituary, careful to not spill a single red drop.

"So, that's what you turned to," Maggie said. "Is that why you're this way? Drugs?"

Nate sneered at the claim. "Hardly," he said, gathering his things. He and opened the security door and growled, "Leave us alone, we don't need you."

"What 'we,' what 'us?' Let all this about Jamie go. Please! For my family. For yourself."

"I don't have to let anything go. It already came back." He kicked the security door shut and disappeared, locking her out.

Maggie pounded the door, shouting, "Jamie's dead, you asshole! Doing this, you only keep killing him over and over and over." She collapsed onto the remaining papers, crying as their beleaguering typefaces reared at her. Although she knew Nate could not hear and was not listening anyway, she rested awhile in the foyer, chokingly repeating for her own respite from the harrowing stories ceaselessly being retold before her, "You keep killing him…you keep killing him…you keep killing him…"

Chapter 14

BUZZZZZZ.

The Loft's gruff front door buzzer ripped the entire second floor as it rang. Its summoner, Linc, was able to hear it all the way from the lobby as they waited to be granted access. They double checked the address jotted on community center stationary, recalling its procurement.

Buzz. Buzz. Buzz.

"Time's up," Linc had clicked their watch. "Reconvene next week?"

The college student patient was about to cap off her story and reach an actualizing epiphany when she said of the news, "Oh, sorry, I didn't mean to spill over. I thought there were five minutes left."

Linc checked the wall clock against their watch. She was correct. There were five minutes left, their brain was the one ahead. They chuckled self-consciously, "Many pardons, my dear, an honest mistake. Please go on."

"No, it's ok, if you have somewhere to be we'll just pick up next week. Our talks have helped keep me afloat so much this semester. You're just so easy to vibe with. So, thank you."

"Well, I'm glad you keep comin' when you need it. I'll do you better and tack an extra ten for us next time."

"Great, bye!"

"Bye."

The therapy space closed. Linc felt awful. She was gushing about her first 'A's after a nervous breakdown and there they were preoccupied on another patient who did not keep coming. Stalking the water cooler in the back offices later, Linc's thoughts slid to the bunkers of file cabinets along the wall. Ensuring no one was around, they yanked open the drawer marked 'A-E' and went hunting.

BUZZZZZZZ.

Access granted.

Knock.

Knoc

Kno...

The resolve in Linc's knocking on Nate's door fell flat. Unauthorized and unethical did not begin to describe being here. Perusing case summaries, copying down confidential personal information and utilizing both for personal means. They were toeing the lines of a lot of laws thought, technically, Linc never swore any type of oath when they entered into practice. Dutiful obligation ingrained throughout upbringing was this visit's impetus. If anyone you cared for dropped out of the social sphere their empty chair at the table would always be missed.

Also, Linc was deeply troubled when Nate did not call to schedule his next session. After his contentious last one, he vanished off the face of the Earth without a trace. No one, even the heartbroken, just does that unless some self-fulfilling fate had befallen them. Nate's fate was left a toss-up since he brought that box in and made Linc's own days just as strange.

Nightmares plagued them of what had happened when they went with Nate toward that box. They were not just any nightmares either. They were visions of blank, plunging chasms that danced with strings…puppet strings…

Get out of your head and get on with this, they thought to bolster themselves.

Knock.

Knoc

Whispery voices arose and conversed behind the door.

One spoke in clear English, "Let me see who it is. If it's not someone we want I'll send them away."

The other spoke in confusing gibberish, "…"

"Yes, dear, I'll be ready soon. Go wait in the living room." There was a pause. Then, Nate boomed, "Who is it?!"

Linc composed themselves. "It's Linc."

"Linc?"

"From the Center. You missed makin' some appointments and I wanted to do a wellness check."

More radio silence.

"I don't usually do this," Linc said. "But I'm real worried about you. You got a minute?"

The quiets in between were unsettling because it felt like the therapist was not the only one doing the analyzing. Dynamics had no power here.

The deadbolt unlatched. Linc was greeted by a sliver through which Nate peeked out, cloaked in shadow. He looked decrepit. Linc tried to keep it positive, "Hey, my friend, how you been? Feelin' ok?"

"Fine."

"Fine. Fine. That's a good thing. Fine. What have you been up to? If I may ask."

"That's not what you want to ask."

"Excuse me?"

"Tell me the real reason you came here."

Linc shrugged.

Nate curled a cruel smile, "Diagnostic minds have the hardest times turning in on themselves. Though I don't have a PHD, I have perception. You came because you're afraid."

"What would I be afraid of?"

"Of our last session. Me being right. Right about us having a more *spirited* discussion. It's probably been bothering you every day, hasn't it? Not sleeping well?"

Linc regretted the impulsive drop-in. This sly man was a hideous imposter. Yes, Linc was afraid. Very afraid. But these words, albeit true, were laced with venom.

"Sit down, Doc," Nate invited Linc. "I'll talk about fear with you."

The way his phrasings bore straight to the soul made it difficult for Linc to decline. Nevertheless, their skin crawled as if it were infested with millipedes as they opted to accept and sit. "I care about you a lot, Nate," they felt compelled to inform, venturing further without thinking, "You're someone to like, I always saw that. Even in a non-therapy sense. I miss caring about you in person."

Behind the slivered door, Nate genuflected. The door creaked open wider and, backwardly, he turned on the balls of his feet and slithered himself upside-down to Linc's level.

Hygiene was being grossly neglected, Linc saw. Offensive odors from greasy body stains and unkempt scruff co-mingled in the damp landing. This was not a sad person. This was not someone suffering through simple emotions. This was an escalation routinely drawn and quartered by torment and anguish.

"We going to chat like good ole boys?" Nate asked them.

Linc faced Nate's poison head on. They would never be reduced to speaking to anyone as anything less, but dredging up how Nate and Linc's hardball was played, their jousts were allowed to be occasionally less than nice, "We are goin' to chat about how you look like shit."

Nate licked his chops. "Thank you for the compliment. I feel like shit too. I'm so happy."

"Happy? This looks pretty unhealthy to me."

Nate winked at them deviously.

Illusionary centipedes, swifter in motion, joined their slower, burrowing counterparts on Linc's skin. They persisted, "I invested six-plus months in counseling you about pathways to take in your relationship, your friendships, your job. Then, when the first got taken away by chance, our labor got harder but we committed to find the way to answers. Does this feel like that progression you *were* amenable to? Even before encountering loss—oh for heaven's sake I'm not sidestepping with you anymore—DEATH? Are you going to accept DEATH?"

"I accept damage," Nate said, cavalier. "Death does that. It damages people. To what extent, I dunno. Most of it is cosmetic but I'm helping to repair all those parts. Everything else, traits and whatever, fall back on their own. As do other perks. So, I don't worry about the physical flaws until they're fixed. Man, how they're fixing though. Resurrection is one hunky master."

All the non-sequiturs weaving around made Linc light-headed.

Nate read their confusion and said with arid eyes, "Puttin' it to you straight as you prefer, I'm saying past relationship problems are pretty pithy when you have a life to rebuild."

Linc exterminated the creepy crawlies and braved the foul stenches to throw some perspective at their rogue client,

"Whose life, yours? What I see is a blatant disrespect for any life including the one that's gone."

Nate gurgled, "It's not gone!"

"Then who else in that apartment with you? I heard another voice."

"Jamie!" Nate hacked, disgusted, and spit up a gob of bile. "I thought your intellect would have figured that out by now."

"There are no such things as ghosts or other dimensions, Nate. I don't believe in any of what you're testing me with."

"Ghosts don't wait for you to believe, they find a way to make you. You virtuosos of healing think you know everything. I'll prove he's here." Nate acrobatically flounced away.

Linc contemplated phoning either for an ambulance with a strait jacket or a priest up for a blessing. Before they could, Nate reemerged on all fours with a crinkled page in his fist.

Nate shook it at them. "See? Jamie's been painting again. You've seen some of his work during our sessions. This is his."

Linc humored Nate and regretted that even more. The piece was a primitive finger painting evocative of Expressionist malice and dread, a far cry from the bright, suave elegance of watercolors.

Nate bargained with Linc to believe him, "I unpacked the box like it had wanted me to. Pieces of Jamie were inside. I was hearing multiple advices, some reliable, some not, yours included, to guide me through my haze. See," Nate explained, inching towards the therapist (who was covertly fumbling for their cell phone), "there's more than just proverbial paths. They're called planes; regions even shrinks can't see. They possess coveted souls but, as the advice led me to, the right dose of reflection and concentration ferried my Jamie back. *He's* the only one who needs help now. To be part of our world again and end this mess. He's getting stronger. Once ready, he promised we'll reset. Start over. Like nothing ever happened."

The sole party being duped by the conceit was Nate, though Linc was no less scared and dismayed. "This is deranged," they said. They attempted dialing 911 through their pocket, not making it past locking themselves out of the passcode screen. A gulp bubbled up in their throat.

This triggered Nate. He curled his fingers to snatch that little gulp right up and said, "Don't take this as a failure, Linc, take it as a lesson."

"..." came faraway sounding gibberish nearby the door. Nate retracted. Linc was cut by the same chill the artwork gave. Jagged bolts of darkness cast under the door's threshold; a blackness so commanding it instantly transfixed them both and vampirically sucked the already dim light out from the landing and into The Loft.

"I'm sorry, mister," Nate submissively groveled to the darkness, "you've been waiting." He rolled up his sleeve. A syringe was dangling, the needle stuck halfway in the crook of his elbow. Nate made his fingers salute and tapped the punctured vein. The vein bulged resentfully. Not to be hampered by his own body, Nate rammed the needle in and drew the plunger. CC's of blood rose to the brim of the vial. Nate plucked the needle out and slipped the drawn ichor with bewitched agony to the beckoning master inside.

Linc heard the most disgusting noises that may have been either *their* imagination or truly was *the darkness* squirting and lapping up the plasma with a needy mouth. Linc was not going to hang around to deliberate the choices.

Nate laughed hoarsely, "A touch of bloodletting is a fair toll for love."

"..." the gibberish croaked moistly.

"Jamie wants to know you if you'd like to come in," Nate relayed brightly. "He says a visitor would be good for us now."

"Turn back before it's too late, Nate," Linc declined. "Whatever's making these promises to you—or if it's yourself doing it—it's not right."

"You once counseled me that there is no right way," Nate said.

Linc admonished themselves of further responsibility, "Our time is up. And I was never here."

They broke away as fast as they could.

Their downward climb lasted an eternity and that was only to the floor below. Linc collapsed unwittingly against another front door. They heard Nate slam his, the latching deadbolt echoing strangely off every wall until enough silence blanketed the stairwell for Linc to try and catch their breath.

* * *

At that very moment, Janelle was in her cubicle answering her umpteenth consecutive phone call of the day without a professional salutation or company recitation. A technical glitch had rerouted scores of hospitality supply orders around the greater city area and spun the entire office into a flurry with a tidal wave call volume of vendors and buyers alike demanding nothing except entitled satisfaction. Expecting another disgruntled talkback, Janelle was elated by the voice on the other line.

"NATE," she exclaimed. "Oh my God, I've been worried sick. It's nuts in here today. What's going on with you?" She strained to listen. "Mmm-hmm, talk louder, honey, I can barely hear you." He sounded so raspy. "You need me to what? Come over?

Absolutely! Of course, I can come see you. Need me to come right now? I'll have to sneak out—oh, tonight. Okay. Sure. You'll be alright until—got it. I will race right over—stay what?" She strained again but Nate disconnected. What an odd thing to say. "You stay hydrated as well," Janelle muttered, hanging up, only to pick up the next call that did turn out to be another disgruntled talkback.

* * *

Linc finally caught their breath when the door they were leaning on went *click* and cracked open. Linc teetered and caught their balance just in time to not bowl this loft's resident over.

"Excuse me," Max inquired suspiciously, "can I help you? Lotta commotion out here."

Linc put space between them. "My sincerest apologies, sir. I was visitin' a…visitin' someone and just got a little light headed. Didn't mean to disturb." They waved sheepishly and started to leave.

"Wait. Were you up there to see Nate?"

"Yes, I was," Linc replied.

"How is he?"

Linc paused, considering. They came up with, "I honestly cannot answer that."

Max could appreciate that answer and agreed, "I feel where you're coming from. How do you know Nate?"

"I'm…an acquaintance. Linc," they offered their hand.

"Max. Nice to meet you."

"Likewise, Max. You're a friend of Nate's, right?"

Max shrugged. "Tried to be. Was more Jamie's. We were

109

art buddies. Worked on stuff together all the time. We were planning a show before he left and then…you know, passed away. We were planning to show off our crafts in a unique, blended way. Still developing some of the photos actually. He was a cool guy."

Linc twinkled. "So I've heard." They enjoyed the respite of witnessing real remembrance. "I hate to take up more time but may I see one of those photographs? If it's no intrusion."

Max lit a bit up, rarely receiving such an invitation. "For sure! Um, wait one sec." He jogged off.

Linc noticed a backpack right inside being prepared for an overnight stay as they waited.

Max returned and held out a print. "Here, this is one of my favorites. It's an outtake, I guess you'd call it, of Jamie in his studio. We were attempting to communicate the life of a watercolorist. The guy had a sense of humor. As you can see, a real pistol too."

Pistol was right. Max's saturated photo portrayed Jamie splayed on the floor whipping a blue-hued—was that *cerulean?*—brush at an oblong canvas already splashed with arches of color. His smile would best be described as infectious. His *joie de vie* was as indivisible from the brightness in the color palette as every recounting Linc had heard.

"That's a beautiful memento," Linc said.

Max murmured, "Yeah. I want it to open the show when it's ready."

"Have you shown any of these to Nate?"

Max was still wrapped up in the reminiscent photo.

The respite had quit, though. The name was not a favorable association for Max, Linc inferred from the alienated silence stemming from of the slightest mention of Nate. Linc rephrased to try and draw it out, "Have you seen Nate lately or checked in on him or…would you?"

"We're not exactly on neighborly terms."

"I only ask because it may be a while for me and I'm afraid—"

"I'm afraid too," Max interrupted. He scooped up a nearby pet crate. Timid eyes peered out the mesh caging. "This is my cat, Mocha. She adored Jamie. They always palled around. After he died, she was pretty rudely unwelcome upstairs. Not for a lack of effort on her part. But, the other night she ran in after being outside—she doesn't wander far—and…look at her side."

Mocha meowed wearily. Unable to tell the full story, she rolled over.

Her patchwork stitching and stapling made Linc queasy. They asked Max warily, "You're not suggesting…?"

"What, some street animal clawed her up? No offense but I'm not trying to begin a session nor can I pinpoint anything but someone did to this to my cat and is downright cruel. Also, whatever is happening on the second floor has been made crystal clearly none of my business." He tried to shut the door on Linc.

"Can you just check on him, Max? I really, truly, can't come back."

"We're actually going out of town to crash at a buddy's pad awhile," Max said nudging the backpack, thus flatlining the conversation. "Not sure when we'll be back. Need some peace and quiet of our own. I'm sorry, I wish I could do more. I have to go give Mocha her pain meds."

Linc gave up. "Fine. I'll call authorities for another wellness check I guess. For Nate's own sake, I hope he realizes to reach out to you. After all, you're the one that took him to the funeral.

That's why I recognized you. Merits a lot having done that for him."

Max uncharacteristically jeered, "Wow, now there's a fucking joke."

The outburst perplexed Linc. "What? I wasn't telling a joke."

"Nate told you I took him to the funeral? That we went together?"

"Yeah."

Max fumed enough to start the next Great Chicago Fire. Linc felt the carpet unraveling out from under them as they awaited Max's reveal of the ultimate insult:

"Nate did not go with me. He did not go with anyone. No. *Nate never even went to Jamie's funeral!*"

V

R.I.P.

Chapter 15

"*Hold still,*" the shadow man might have said. Those were the only discernable phonetics Nate heard in the slipshod delivery. He attempted to ask for repetition but struggled to find a single body part not weakened out of blood loss to do so.

Perched atop the toilet nearby, the shadow man was peering at him through rising puffs of steam, silently drumming twiggy fingers across where the sketchpad in its lap ought to have been. It was trying to convey annoyance. The way its puttied scar tissue features wrenched between a frown and a grin stifling a chuckle, however, came across more as perturbed. The grotesque look was not adorable, yet not unfamiliar to Nate. SOMEONE was being uncooperative about SOMETHING.

About what this time around, though, vexed Nate. He was submerged in the balmy bathwater, readying to pose. Why the agitation?

But there was no time for puzzling. Impatient at just being gawked at, the shadow man jabbed its twiggy fingers forward. "*I said: HOLD STILL,*" it pronounced wetly. "*You promised.*"

Nate was about to try his limbs harder only to discover he was not at incredible odds with the present Moment, just on delay. This was The Moment he was waiting for and he could move within it! Harnessing this twist in agency, Nate signaled his fully clothed self to laze and, on pins and needles, anticipated the exact chain of events that would culminate with his and the entity's multi-planar intervention in the course of time and life itself. Everything was about to change!

The shadow man smirked with context and, before long, all out smiled. With what was construed as a cheeky, *"Thank you,"* it turned its attentions away to a collection of stainless-steel razor blades spread across the sink.

Nate drifted into comfortable repose. He had done everything there was to be done. He was not helpless. He was there in full control.

He thought.

To be part of this new Moment, a deep recess in his psyche icily informed him, *you will have all mortal devices at your disposal and will be conscious, no longer a pinned fly on the wall, until you are sacrificed by the perspective you chose to remain with no kind regards for stopping. Or caring.*

This was not how The Moment went!

The compromise was utterly distasteful to Nate and contrary to how everything was inscribed in history. Nate draped an arm over the side of the tub, his composition that of a martyr dying from his own cause, and blearily asked the shadow man, "Aren't you supposed to paint me, Jamie? Then you're supposed to stay. We agreed."

The shadow man grumbled and selected a long, fresh blade and clamped it between its own razor-sharp baby teeth like a primeval game hunter. Nate saw himself in the blade as the shadow man scrutinized him with a keen once over, slurring, *"You paint me. You die alone."*

Nate had no time to react. The shadow man grabbed the

blade. Arced it high in the air. And swung.

The blade stopped by mere hairs on Nate's throat as pattering footsteps passed outside the bathroom door. Backing the razor off, the shadow man snarled contemptuously. It crookedly staggered up, poised to sleuth for whomever was disturbing this Moment. Before doing so, however, it regarded Nate and slurred again, *"You're not freed."*

Slamming Nate's head against the ceramic, it threw open the door and darted away.

Nate felt his skull twinge as he sank into the tub. The door closed on its own. The pressure in The New Moment warbled as memory and time mixed and matched.

The wall spat plaster. Spidery threads of viridian pooled from the resulting cracks, crawling out of them in vines. The wall itself wavered as if it were being washed away or...

Jamie's abstraction, the kaleidoscope, abruptly materialized before Nate, rocking on the edge of the tub. The blush pinks and jaunty yellows on its face lent amazing optimism to the bizarre scene. But the overflowing sadness of evening blues and royal purples in and around its pouting lips betrayed a notion that the worst *had* come. It swung around towards the sullied bathwater, unfurling its like angels' wings, and lithely slid onto Nate's lap to embrace him.

The kaleidoscope proffered a kiss and leaned in, so closely, to give it.

What had fallen before by the damnable Wayside of broken memories filled in:

Jamie pressed Nate with the greatest lips ever known. Their soft, plush curvature coaxed Nate's head to tilt and slide downward as

Jamie locked in and slid his tongue in and around. Jamie passionately held the French kiss until both of them had submerged themselves. Next, like a life preserver, Jamie floated the two of them back up and slicked the water off them both. Sniffling, he gazed at Nate adoringly then climbed out to begin gathering up his supplies. He said to Nate, "Thanks for sitting for my gr-AHND portrait, darling. It's already my favorite. I'm going to keep it at my new desk to remind me how pretty you are. Prettiest guy I can think of. Especially when you're relaxed. I'm going upstairs to dry off and go to bed. Get some rest before the big drive tomorrow. You stay here, enjoy the bath. Don't wait up. I'll see in the morning."

In the tub, through a curtain of water, Nate watched the kaleidoscope walk away. In its hand was the sketchpad, the unrevealed, finished painting wedged inside. Turning back for one last Moment, it added to him distantly and presciently, *"Promise you won't hate me, Nate. I'll come back, I swear."* The kaleidoscope nodded to Nate and delivered a timid, one-handed bye-bye as it stole for the door. The water-colored body began to shred apart from the inside-out as it stepped to the adjoining hallway...

No.

...hoisting two tall, oblong objects:

No!

Suitcases.

The door slammed with a resounding BOOM—

Mercilessly, the water flooded in and drowned everything...

...including Nate's lungs.

—to **black.** To neon red. Then hazy, rippling grey as puppet strings fought to grab hold.

Shrill, wailing screams blasted The Loft.

Chapter 16

Nate mightily arose, panicked, coughing and thrashing, immediately stricken with incredible, insurmountable déjà vu.

The bathroom was empty. Absent of color. Nobody on the toilet. Nothing at all changed.

Stop playing the fool, common sense urged above the steamy clouds of deception. *Everything has changed.*

Nate massaged where he felt the common sense and other mindful urgencies clawing at the fugue infecting his impacted head. He saw double as he heaved himself out of the bathtub, nearly crumpling under the weight of his sopping clothes. He rained all across the tile floor, gritty bathwater seeping out his orifices. He leaned, wobbly legs astride, against the sink. In his shifting vision, he stepped into a hall of mirrors where he discovered a reflection of himself that was of him the night, weeks prior, he brought the box and its gateways home to The Loft.

"Don't you have anything better to show me," the reflection whined, mockingly chastising him for even mulling something else.

The mirror image distorted as Nate feebly scrubbed off the steam. In the stranger's place replaced his real, waxen and bloodshot face. He plied at his horrendous visage. His balance still shaky, his leg brushed the toilet seat and he stumbled and noticed a piece of paper awaited him. Nate raised it, aware that he had seen this at least twice before: first when it was completed and taken away and, second, when it was returned and fished out from the box.

Jamie's signature and heart icon were scribbled in the bottom corner of the Zen watercolor of Nate gracefully rendered nude in the tub.

"The last moment," Nate consciously said, "you promised me you'd come back." Bearing to regard the evidence of such happening, he felt so incredibly guilty. "What have I done," he asked rhetorically?

Thud. Thunk. THUD!

Nate was stolen out of the entire stupor by a muted clamor happening elsewhere in The Loft. He hesitated, fearful. Forcing his vision to line up single file, he opened the door to seek the answer to his question.

Nate was greeted by a majestic thicket of fog rolling through the air. He swatted the unearthly drift and blindly guided himself out of the bathroom. The mist was cool, sending his teeth to chattering. The floorboards creaked and squished under his heavy, water-logged steps. Outlines of furniture and furnishings emerged in the shady living room, but no moving figures. Only the touch lamps, the twin objects of Nate and Jamie's whimsies, were blinking in the clouds. Up and up and off and up again. Their bulbs illuminated rapidly like beacons warning sailing ships of treachery.

"Hello," Nate called. "Who's in there? Anybody? I heard you. I did! I'm done imagining everything. I think…"

The Loft answered secretively.

Rattle rattle rattle, flapped the windows.

Hissssssssssss CLANK, went the spine crunching radiator.

Whimp—, a soft, cut off unknown.

And then there were none in the hushed wilderness.

Soon, after moments of silence, the tinny plucks of a harp from the lofted above drew Nate to the stairs. He stopped at the bottom step leading up to the bedroom and stared. The inexorable truth grew in his belly that the confusing déjà vu would soon give way to clarity if he climbed and that this climb would be his last.

If he dared.

Abandon all hope, all ye who enter here, the descent Nate allowed himself to take had warned.

Taking the first steps to reclamation, Nate ascended mountainous Limbo. The guilt in him roiled and sad, wincing pains tore at his chest. Coupled with sagging clothes, he was debilitated halfway. Nate peeled off the wretched garments. He stripped article by article until he was stark naked. The burden and the pains lifted some. Upon reaching the summit, the billows of the fog began to part and were banished altogether as Nate fell into his bedroom and back through the looking glass.

He immediately swore bloody Hell. Track marks and bruised entry points trailed his arms. Used, blood-soaked syringes littered the floor. Mussed, blood-stained bed sheets made up the bed. Size eight, bloodied footprints were everywhere. Everything was one bloody affair.

A patiently open book waited by the banister at Nate's feet. He picked it up and resumed reading what Astrid O'Toole's thrift shop <u>Guide</u> had wanted him to all along:

Chapter 12
PHANTASMA

Creatures of the abyss deserve no introduction, yet here I go. Aforementioned in the previous chapter, predators lurk within the planar walls of the Unknown. They are repugnant, twisted and vile abominations known in simpler terms as: PHANTASMS.

When a mortal being dies, they release energy, positive and negative. These energies are discarded about the nether-sphere with eternal potential to formulate other-worldly beings, most common examples being apparitions, poltergeists or premonitory feelings. Some energies are able to co-mingle peacefully, others are unwanted like garbage. Phantasms are birthed from the detritus of the latter form.

Phantasms seek to trick the misguided living into accepting them back to the real world, often hiding themselves behind the varieties of positive energies that draw other, more intended spirits toward us. Their missions are singular: to viciously sap and destroy the life of a host through empty promises, its goal to reclaim flesh and, as it regains power, unceasingly attempt to spread its putrid lies beyond the borders of its initial target.

Once afflicted by a phantasm there is almost no going back. I was fortunate. I wish the same upon you, skeptic, for I am not heartless.

Since you have now chosen to heed, I shall expound.

Those were her last words. The remaining had been ripped spine to stern.

Nate dropped the dismembered text, arriving next at Jamie's desecrated studio. The shrine's effects were mangled up in piles and snapped to pieces. Nate set his watercolor portrait on the rubble with shallow gasps, hoping and, in an act he was rarely moved to, praying he had not committed these acts.

Denial was futile, which brought him to the shattered mirror.

Nate delicately lifted the object of his gazes. Deep, splintered claw marks zig-zagged out both sides of the frame. The injured shards spread around the desk had the most listless of shines. Something had come out and stolen all their joy.

Hatred, Nate realized. Hatred did this. The one promise Jamie had asked him to make, Nate had broken. Looking last at the diabolical script on the wall, the picture was clear.

Everything seemed so easy.

Nate hopelessly cradled his face, having not only broken the promise but wrought something horrid from it. He sobbed into his palms, "I'm sorry, Jamie, oh fuck I'm sorry! I should have just let you go. Every chance you gave…I should have let you go. You didn't deserve this. I didn't deserve you."

A lone, shimmering orb blossomed from one of the severed brushes. It was the last of the symphony's survivors not suffocated by the despair that overwhelmed The Loft. The orb danced Nate's cheek. Nate jumped and was amazed by the pinprick of energy hovering before him.

"Jamie," he said wistfully. "That's you. You did come back."

As nothing more, as nothing less, Nate understood. *But what was the rest of this?*

Unfinished business, Janelle's voice reminded. *Energies exist in the world. They exist in different forms and it's your choice how to open up to them and how to fix them if they're broken. Just don't expect them to go by any rule book.*

124

"Janelle," Nate muttered. Her advice had cropped up not just for memory's sake. There was another reason Nate could not quite put his finger on…

Hahahahahahahahahahahahahahahahahahahahahahahahaha

The ghoulish cackling came behind him. Nate grimaced. He swayed around and lumbered to the railing. There, the cosmic charade ended. Hanging upside-down from the ceiling oozing oily essence, black as midnight, was Nate's haunting shadow man.

The fraud.

The negative.

The sin.

The phantasm.

And dangling in its grasp by the ankle, gagged and bound, was Janelle.

"Don't you dare hurt her," Nate screamed.

The phantasm screeched, dissatisfied by all these rude intrusions on its need to feed.

"Put her down! You have no business with her."

Having gleaned enough in its brief existence, the phantasm aped the sass of its deceased counterpart and exaggeratingly cocked a coy head. It had time for a game. Hunger games toughen up meat. The phantasm jeered and bobbed Janelle like a toy. She whimpered through her dish towel gag. Clotted bite marks rung her neck.

This beast was not to be underestimated. Nate saw the potentially fatal mistake of doing so as the phantasm simply did what he demanded and released Janelle into straight freefall. Nate swung himself about the banister and barreled down the stairs. Janelle was already feet from crashing headlong into the coffee table. Tensing every fiber of potential in his calves, Nate launched a leap of faith to save her. The lone orb of Jamie snuck up behind and lent him a propelling shove with the last of its near-extinct energy, popping into tiny stars as it dissipated.

Nate reached out his arms. By the thickly knitted threads of her sweater, he nabbed Janelle and hugged her horizontally. With only a dent to the frame and a bounce up, they landed miraculously unharmed on the couch.

Quickly, Nate undid Janelle's bindings. She gratefully dislodged the gag herself and sucked in starved breaths. Nate checked her for injuries asking, "Janelle, my friend, is anything hurt? Are you alright?"

She shook her head. "No, I'm not alright but nothing's hurt except my neck! The front door was open when I got here and something grabbed me and—are you ok?! You're naked and cut to pieces."

"Don't worry about me, not for a long, long time. I'm the one that got you into this."

Janelle couldn't help herself, "Oh, so you remember talking to me this time."

"Yeah, a lot's getting remembered and it's all a fiasco."

The ceiling creaked and their reunion became short-lived. The phantasm backflipped and crunched to the living room floor, growling and towering over them. The sinews of its exposed musculature were furiously wriggling like spasmodic earthworms.

"You put that mildly," Janelle said petrified.

The phantasm snatched both of them by the skull crown and squeezed to squash. Nate grit his teeth under the pressure. He swung wild, retaliatory punches and that were rebounded by a padded epidermis of ectoplasm. The phantasm displayed not the slightest bit of hurt, only humor at their plight.

Smears of Janelle's neck wound had wiped from Nate's hand to the phantasm's abdomen. Judging the phantasm's fleshy knots of wriggling sinews closer, Nate watched their throes intensify as they absorbed Janelle's blood the same way they had done with his own unpleasant donations. They were the engines of its hunger, the vulnerable sucklers driving its force. He needed to go deeper.

Nate aimed for the knots and swung hard. His fist buried in gut and twisted in goop. The phantasm wrenched away, mortified by the sudden leak disrupting its belly. Janelle followed Nate's cue and grabbed the phantasm's arm, going for broke with a sinking bite to a bunch of chewy veins.

The phantasm crumpled and crawled, scaling the wall and snaked right through the slats of a heating vent. Its presence hissed along the maze of pipes, bursting every air bubble in its path with diminishing

CLANK

Clank

clanks...

Reprieve.

Janelle spat out vile bile. Nate, slathering the slimy ecto on the couch cushion, regarded her with astonishment.

She shrugged. "What? I'm a biter."

"You don't need to do this," Nate said. "I don't know to what extent yet, but I think I've hurt enough people already and cannot let you be another. Save yourself."

Janelle shook her head. "We're going to save each other. What you're fighting cannot be fought alone. I think you got enough proof of that. Never thought I'd see the day something I deigned to believe as a campfire story was actually real."

Nate tugged at his hair, nearing hysterics, "It made me promises. Promises I should have known were bait. I should have seen right through it but I was so fucking selfish every step of the fucking way that anything I could do to kick death in the fucking teeth for taking away what I also so fucking selfishly clung to just because I didn't want anything to ever change…I'm no better. I'm just as guilty and need to face the consequences."

Janelle slapped him in the jaw. "Snap out of it! Dying is natural. It's going to happen to me, to you and everyone we know. And if this is it now, so be it. But there's a sanctity to dying, at least for me, and that thing is the pure definition of sacrilege. You see what it's done. It's all over your body! Nothing can change the past, Nate. Ghosts are no exception. They can help you at least change your future. Saying as your friend, this is messed the Hell up but I have no hard feelings because the one thing that cannot exist anywhere except in our world…is forgiveness."

"What if I'm past forgiveness?"

"No one is past forgiveness. You just have to put in the hard work…starting now with putting this thing back where it came from. Now, how the fuck are we going to do that?"

Hiss. Air, both hot and cold, blew out of the vent.

Nate raced to the bathroom to arm himself with one of the razor blades on the sink. He glanced at the mirror, chewed his lip, and returned to Janelle. "We have to scry," he started to explain.

"Scry?"

"That's what I did to see Jamie. It's divination, looking past a reflective surface to, in turn, be reflected a vision of what you're looking for. It's like opening a door to The Other Side. Problem is, as you witness, leaving that door wide open means what you're seeing sees you and can exit. That's why when I saw Jamie he kept looking over his shoulder. He was afraid of what was behind him. He was trying to protect me and even himself."

"So, you need to gaze and let another vision cross this back through then shut the damn door."

"And never open it again."

"Where to then? We need to act fast."

Nate thought. All the supplies were on Jamie's desk. However. "The bathroom," he said, "the mirror the phantasm used in the bedroom was smashed. Probably so it could not be sent back. There's only one choice. We need to go get the candles and lure it—"

Before he could finish there was a great rumble in the kitchen. Side by side, Nate and Janelle crept forward together. Nate readied the razor. There was another shake, this time from the kitchen sink. Pressure was mounting underneath it from a whole other set of pipes.

CLANK!

The sink exploded in a spray of water and fixtures. The faucet shot Janelle in the ribs and knocked her flat. The water pressure reeled Nate into the kitchen island.

The shifty phantasm stretched out from the plumbing, enraged. It chopped Nate in the shoulder to disarm him of the blade and retrieved it for itself. It snaked out and vaulted through the air to place Nate in a chokehold, somersaulting him over the island and onto the floor. On his knees, Nate sputtered as several scabs started to reopen. The phantasm stuck out a wagging tongue and slurped at the refreshments.

The blood slid across newly generated flesh, particularly its neck where flaps of muscle and skin flayed apart to reveal vocal cords that coiled together and birthed a mature voice box.

The cords vibrated. Rich, formulated words boomed rather than garbled, "Why do you struggle so? If you want this to end so badly let it end quickly while you still have the chance! We agreed!"

Nate gasped, "You're a monster. I should never have agreed. I want you gone!"

The phantasm tightened its grip, crushing Nate's windpipe. "Fine. I know it is Jamie you wanted. Give me the flesh I want and I will banish myself entirely. In return, I'll put you with Jamie forever. I can do that. You know my power."

Nate considered, the overwhelming charisma of the promises still appealing.

"Nate, no, don't bargain with it," Janelle warned, sitting up from the floor.

Nate glared at the phantasm, "How do I know you're telling the truth?"

The phantasm purred, "Because I see the truth and you never even read or went to it."

Tears welled in Nate's eyes. In this bargain, there would be two victors but to only one would go the spoils.

Janelle's plea faded to the background, "Nate, you do not need to do it this way!"

Nate turned to Janelle crying and said, "Run." She stared back at him, shocked. Looking away before she could protest, Nate prostrated himself before the phantasm. The malevolence loosened its hold, pleased. Nate offered his wrists and made one last stipulation, "Only take me to the truth. Let her and anyone else I involved go."

The phantasm chortled, "I promise." It swung the razor blade and slashed. Blood raced forth from Nate's pulsing arteries. The phantasm pressed eager fingers into the wounds.

Nate, wrists afire, screamed and was lost in a searing, white hot light.

* * *

Cruising the expressway at 70mph around one in the morning, the wind was sailing through Jamie's hair while thumping R&B beats rocked the rental car. The suitcases were in the back seat. His satchel was snugly by his hip, the paint brushes poking at him playfully. He was smiling.

In a stunning instant, a drunken imbecile abruptly veered many lanes too far and cut Jamie off. Jamie swerved the rental car's steering wheel, tires squealing as he bashed the cement barricade, ricocheting back over to the approaching SUV behind him. The SUV, unable to slam the brakes fast enough, broadsided and flipped the rental completely over in a flood of high beams and bursting shrapnel.

The seat belt suspended the motionless Jamie in his seat. Contusions were instantaneous across his body. Forceful impact concaved multiple organs including his brain. He voided over the favorite watercolor-stained tee shirt he was wearing. His right hand had slipped into the satchel, somehow still snugly at his side, and clutched its contents, notably the watercolor portrait of Nate.

He was smiling.

Sirens wailed in the distance.

Nate, placed in the scene by the phantasm, fell back from the passenger seat. He was the uninjured bystander of this vision but still stripped and profusely bleeding from the real elsewhere. He looked, horrified, over at the facts pouring out as they did in the disregarded accident report. He wanted to cradle and comfort his poor boyfriend even it meant nothing to the corpse. It would have least meant Nate tried. He could have shown Jamie how un-resentful he really was. How much he cared.

Now it was too late. Both blood-drenched and battered, it was time to resign. Nothing more to say, Death was the winner reaping it all.

There were dull thumps against the mangled vehicle's frame. Clumps of dirt sifted past the fractured windshield and windows. It thickened, joined by roots and rocks, and piled up around the car, rapidly beginning to crush the cabin and leak inside. Earthworms and dung beetles skittered out from the dirt, their wriggling feelers avidly arriving on both bodies to start the delicious process of decomposition. Prevented initially by weakness, the elements and earth separated Nate from Jamie in their joint casket, eternally divided. Nate's eyes slowly closed. At least they were together.

Sirens wailed in the distance.

A man approached on the asphalt, reaching out a searing white light of his own.

* * *

Nate's sight shunted back to a slit of reality. His condition critical, he could hardly feel. His starved veins were a desperate shade of blue under his pale, translucent skin. His heart wanted to pump in reverse to divert the river of siphoning blood but the well was nearly too dry to continue mattering and the new host too strong. The phantasm's material existence was full-fledged: a classical, clay-colored, rippled-muscle minion of the Inferno accented by dually elongated incisor teeth, goblin-y ears and a pair of infant wings flapping out of the cocoon in its back, ready to fly the beast away to farther, greater pastures of evil.

From the opposite end of The Loft, a whip of actual white light cracked against the phantasm's wrists. Sizzles like burning acid on skin bubbled the phantasm's new skin. It howled in distress and, pivoting, ejected itself from the bloodbath.

Nate collapsed, contorting to see who (or what) had crossed over to lash the demon.

The man was elderly and draped in a billowy, grey cloak. Waves of scraggly white locks danced over his milky, blind eyes. His apparition exuded antiquity, experience and a lot of ghostly tentacles. It was the grand priest of poetry, Virgil, back to navigate another Comedy.

Virgil croaked derisive Latin epithets at the phantasm. He stretched the reach of his tentacles toward the creature's wide-open trap, mashed its tongue against its teeth and placed it in a gagging headlock. The phantasm struggled uselessly.

Virgil used the phantasm's weak moment to look at Nate, inner sight searing through the blindness. His native tongue translated itself for Nate to comprehend, "Through the great planes, many noble intentions trek. The perilous seeds belonging to love are sown, only to raise the greatest wreck. Atone, sir, atone." Then, quoting in Italian his epic companion Dante, "Haste denies all acts their dignity."

And, with due diligence, Virgil sprouted his own tongue to launch and wrap around the phantasm's waist and reeled it in. The phantasm flapped its baby wings pitifully. Coming toe to toe with Virgil, both forms began to melt like wax, fusing into one another. Virgil kneed the phantasm and fell the unbonded rest of it. The phantasm clawed up the floorboards as it was dragged through The Loft toward the bathroom, receding into

Virgil's ectoplasm along the way.

Janelle leapt out, a blazing candle in her grasp. She stared stupefied at the strange scry she had summoned and sidestepped it as both creatures wrestled past her in a jumbled knot. A sucking whoosh later, they were out of mortal sight. Janelle blew out the candle, jumped back in and used the holder to smash the bathroom mirror, the last possible portal in The Loft, to pieces.

Salvaging any clean towels from the wreckage of the kitchen, Janelle knelt beside Nate and applied them as a makeshift tourniquet to his wrists. Nate wordlessly apologized to his surroundings with streaming tears. Though thoroughly shaken, Janelle warmly wiped them away.

"Just accept it," she said.

Nate held the hardest breath of his life and expelled all resistance. "I accept," he whispered.

The friends embraced resiliently. Outside, wailing sirens turned down the block, speeding emergency responders that, soon, were to come knocking at Nate's front door.

Chapter 17

One month later.

Nate and Linc met at the opposing pillars of Graceland Cemetery's main gate. It was an overcast, mid-Autumn day. The nip in the air made their shoulders hunch and hands bunch in their coats. They stood feet apart. A moat of silence flowed between them. Both were surprised the other had come.

Nate waded in and met them in the middle. "Hi," he said, "thanks for meeting me."

"I didn't have any appointments, so…you're welcome," Linc replied, standing still. "May I ask why here?"

"I wanted to take a walk."

"In a cemetery? Strange place for a walk."

"There's something in here I need to see and I owe it to you to have you by my side."

Linc tacitly considered. In the doctorate world, indebted gratitude rarely paid back. It was not expected to be. Aid was aid no matter who the person or what the outcome. This one had been written off a lost cause. Linc, however, could not help feeling the need to see this case through not only because of how warped it had become, but of how uniquely personal it was.

Given how inexplicably frightening later personal encounters were, too, Linc was amazed Nate was even standing.

Nate dug his heels, knowing full well Linc was reviewing the recent past that had besmirched his reputation. He reasoned, "You're not wrong if you're wanting to say no. I'm not fooling myself thinking you came out of altruism. You just know the most and, what you don't know...well, I shouldn't be the only one getting closure."

The confidence, however haunted, with which Nate spoke struck Linc. They at least owed him the benefit of the doubt for presenting, by his own volition, such a forward sense of self. This was not the same Nate, of any kind. Peering at the forked roads that led into the deadlands, Linc found imbued in them a mutual mood for discovery and decided to trust Nate.

"Let's stroll," they said.

* * *

Was this Paradise?

The acreages of pastoral, landscaped park stretched in variants of flattened plains and secluded, forested hideaways. Vibrantly green blades of grass defiantly thrived in the autumn chill. Their singular, fresh-cut scent made the air fresh and pure. There were no daisies pushing up, as they had already died for the season, so only tombstones remained to cultivate the landscape. Many of them dated as far back as the early 19th-century when the Great Fire had purged other regions of the city of its resting places and forced inhabitants to move. Unimaginable numbers of souls were displaced in the process which would explain a great deal of Chicago's urban legends and folklore. Over the passages of time, most seemed to have finally settled in their Victorian-style plots and historic monuments.

The land was so quiet. Tranquil. One could have a picnic here.

Linc admired the artisanal craftsmanship of the headstones as they walked. The ones not yet eroded by the elements had their own distinctive markings or cultural iconography; extensions of who lied beneath. Near the cemetery's epicenter, there was a clustered field of markers with no particular sort or distinguishable identities. Linc wondered if it was more a mass plot: an overflow trench with nothing left underneath. Each cemetery has its anomalies. People truly do go missing when they die and sometimes only a suggested memory carries their torch. Catching a glimpse of the miles-long enclosures bordering the cemetery, Linc noticed the wrought iron spear points atop the brick and mortar. They were war-like. Protective.

Aside from keeping the vandals and vagrants out, why such a violent precautionary symbol? What else were they guarding? Isn't this hallowed ground where everyone went to Heaven? Or is it presumptuous that all buried souls reach Heaven? Perhaps being anonymous or well-known have no bearing on the struggle of attaining Perfection? Assuming there was Perfection? What if this cemetery, and others like it, were simply facades or imitations of Paradise to preserve and watch over the virtuous intentions of believing there is only one direction after death while the truth was as vast and sidewinding as the sidewalks here?

So many questions trampled Linc at once. They never felt so rationally lame as these past few months.

With Nate, they turned down a lane of ramshackle mausoleums and suddenly perceived a chalky form in one of the tombs watching them through its squat, rusty gates. As quickly as the form appeared, it flickered and vanished but left the metal gate gently rattling.

Am I sightseeing or seeing sights?

No textual discourse could save Linc from these inquiries and it made them uncomfortable to continue indulging what they were convinced were fantasies. The form, though, had presence and left an indelible impression on Linc. Not a sad one. Or mad. Just a sublime content with being open ended.

"I told you I shouldn't be the only one getting closure," Nate said off the cuff, swerving his eyes on the bending walkway ahead.

Linc took it as a deliberate jab. "Is that why you brought me here? To take advantage of my disbelief and trick some sort of a point on me?"

Nate blinked, truthfully unaware of his tone. "No, no, no," he rushed to explain.

"You're right that I did not have to come. You fuckin' scared me, Nate. Not to mention that you flat out lied during our time. A lot. I'm still not even sure I have a nuanced explanation for anything you've pit me against. Just because I'm a therapist—your ex-therapist, I remind you—does not mean I'm bound to muse on the undead or the possessed or whatever in lieu of a solution I once offered in an office that I know I was comfortable with and knew could help."

"You're right," Nate exclaimed. He shook, trembling. "That's exactly why you and I are both here. You wanted me to confront one of the many faces of grief and I have faced many of them that sanity teaches us are not real. I know some of them are now whether I should or not. They're complicated. I get that. There's a face here, though, that both of us can see. I just need a few more minutes to find it."

Something crumpled in Nate's hand. Linc spied a balled-up cemetery map with coordinates written in the margin. Linc checked their pride to remember Nate's position in relation to their own. They were both still swimming in uncharted waters.

Nate muttered, "I'm sorry. I'm ashamedly new to this."

"We're all new to strange things and in that there is no shame," Linc admitted.

Nate half-smiled, thankful and let comfortable wordlessness pass by a few tombs before breaking more ice lurking below the waters, "Did you call the cops to come by The Loft?"

"Yup," was the curt response.

"Thought so."

"Wellness checks are most logical in our profession when fear overcomes explanation. And what I can't explain logically or Biblically, pullin' from my distant, Southern upbringin', I run from. One of my own ashamed weaknesses."

"You can't fix everything, Linc."

"I have to try otherwise I feel like a failure."

"You didn't fail me. I have a new therapist now and she's say nothing in life can stay unbroken, we just have to work at keeping the pieces together the best we can."

"Sounds like a platitude. Guess we are all the same. Glad you found someone else to talk to."

"Yeah, I think we reached our ethical plateau. Even though…I liked you too. You always saw me for who I was and put up with my crap. Not just because it was your job. I was lucky to meet you. If it were a different timeline…" He deserted the thread there.

Linc tried to ignore the butterflies the dangling thought awoke. So they unspooled another thread, "Speakin' of talkin', what in the Hell did you tell the police when they showed up?"

Nate stifled a pained giggle. "I've never tried to explain so much in so little a way so quickly. You didn't see the place. Or us. Janelle was there. She helped do most of the talking. The EMTs patched me up outside in the ambulance."

"Patched you up?"

Nate rolled back his jacket and revealed the bandages sheathing his wrists.

The implied slash wounds startled Linc, "Oh fuck, Nate. Are they healed?"

"They're healed. I'm not ready to show any scars yet. Too many questions and no one is ready for the answers. So please do not ask."

Linc held up their pinkie finger to swear and left it at that.

Nate turned both of them after reaching the signpost signaling Row 128. They stepped onto the grass. Nate counted.

One. Two. Three. Four. Five. Six. Seven—

Nate stopped and said to Linc proudly, "I actually moved out of The Loft earlier this week. Thought it was time to reinvent myself. Grow up. Make a better home in a modest one bedroom for everything and everyone to settle. Nothing crazy, nothing special. Has enough room."

"In case you have a date," Linc teased.

"Eventually..."

Too far. Linc dialed it back and asked, sensitively, "Think Jamie's there with you?"

"He's right here."

Row 128, Plot 8. A modest, monochromatic marker inscribed 'Beloved Son.'

Linc instinctively took Nate's hand. Nate did not try to push it away.

Nate eulogized impromptu, "Hi, Jamie. Sorry it took so long, I was lost getting here. And that's my last apology because I don't know how many more I should give. You did not choose to die. How could you? You chose to go to school to be the best painter in the world. You belonged there. You were going to come back better. Smarter. Hipper. Happier. I wasn't happy but if I had kept it going, I would have been. We would have been. Instead we chased each other apart because dreams weren't following through. We didn't have to be perfect and we weren't the idyllic couple. But we were good."

Nate's hand slid from Linc's and he fell to his knees, knocking out tears that splotched the limestone.

Nate sobbed, "I can't change anything. Nothing, no matter what it says, can change anything. You were there with me the whole time and I ignored you. I pushed you away because I couldn't cope with losing you. I chose so wrongly and hurt so many people. I tarnished—destroyed—you by believing I could bend the rules for myself. Your family hates me. Max too. Rightfully so. I still have to find some way to mend that. I will. But this is not about me anymore. I'm here for you, my special, beautiful prince."

Out of his jacket, Nate pulled a watercolor brush, the last of the unbroken, and an empty sketchpad and set it on the grave where flowers usually go.

"This is for your art because I know that you are undisturbed here and can work without interruptions. Thank you for all your generosity. Thank you for all the fun. I love you. I miss you. I don't hate you. And I promise…I'll come back. In the meantime, if you ever want to visit, I'll see you at my new home and just leave it at feeling good about sharing even a fraction of time together."

Nate did not say goodbye. He kissed the headstone passionately on the face and ran.

Linc respectfully held back. They were so proud of Nate and so overwhelmed by Jamie, someone they had never met. Still pondering in clichés, *that is the power of true love*. Linc grazed the corner of the stone with their finger as if to shake hands with the deceased and said, "It is an honor and a pleasure to meet you at last, Jamie." They turned to join and comfort Nate, who was crying beside a tree.

The sound of scratching against the headstone stopped Linc. They inhaled deeply and saw their breath mistily exhale. The weather was not that cold. They were at the precipice of acknowledgment; the gates of closure all questions lead to when people are finally ready for them to be opened.

Linc faced Jamie's grave. On the sketchpad, written in mud, was:

The pleasure is all mine.

Linc daintily tore the message off the pad, moved but not astounded. The infinite cemetery around them now held infinite possibilities. A low rumbling quaked on the horizon and Linc felt themselves slip through the seconds of passing time. The eerie sensation of being watched tingled their skin. Peering up at the tree they saw themselves staring back with a secretive smile before they turned to Nate and consoled him with a hug.

The rumble ended and Linc was in the hug. Dazed by the sudden change in perception, they checked over Nate's shoulder, spotting no one. They connected in the embrace, taking comfort that both of them could melt together and be there for one another. It was just as Nate described when they somehow met on that strange level past conscious reasoning.

Time, people, places, objects—they are never what they seem, especially when your emotions are gapingly wide for you and them to crawl through. And there is not a single, humanly way to solve their riddles.

That is the power of ghosts, Linc concluded and pulled away from the hug. Nate's tears had dried, leaving him a puffy, red mess. Linc offered a graciously accepted sleeve to clean some of it up.

"Thank you, Linc," Nate said.

"No, thank you," Linc said softly. They reached out and swept a clump of Nate's mussed hair away from his hazel eyes. Freedom was a handsome look for him. Something was exchanged between them, the grave and their Moment and Linc was certifiably excited to discover what it was.

Nate fell serenely under Linc's touch onto the tree bark and asked shyly, "What do we do now, doc?"

Linc chuckled. "I am plum out of expert testimony. However, I would not mind hangin' a while. Walk around. Explore. Talk. Just as you and I, undefined by rules and roles. Only if you're up for it, though."

"No rules. No roles." How perfect. "Can we meet on the 'veranda' like before?"

Brilliant, yellow sunshine beamed between them even if it was not in the actual sky.

Linc nodded and said, "Yes, let's."

Waving to Row 128, Plot 8, Nate pushed off the tree and strolled alongside Linc. They grinned at one another. Nate wanted to hold their hand again yet decided to wait, smartly learning from rash choices. There was healing left to complete between them and others. Time allotted for pursuit would manifest later, if it were actually right and to be.

Right now, as Nate and Linc rounded a bend leading to the deeper bowels of the cemetery, they allowed the bowing trees to envelope and gobble up their sense of direction.

They ditched the manmade path for the unsteady terrain of the dead and started to converse about this and that; moving on to find the better place they were slowly carving out for themselves in the undeclared hopes that one day, eventually, they too would rest in peace.

About the Author

The sweetest gay gorehound in the Midwest, **Aaron Eischeid** is a native Iowan residing in Chicago with his charmer of a gecko, Gavin. When not found at his day job or in the Paradigm Shift Productions office, he wanders, he bakes or gleefully tries to scare you to death. Angel to some. Demon to others.

You can connect with me on:
🌐 https://paradigmshiftprods.wordpress.com
📘 https://www.facebook.com/paradigmshiftprods

Also by Aaron Eischeid

**AVERSION: A ZINE OF THERA-
PEUTIC VIGNETTES**
A five-part anthology zine, **AVER-
SION** is a queerly surreal work of
freeform horror storytelling featuring
a unique multimedia build and original
illustrations to bring to life the harrowing tale of Owen, a teenager hurled
head and soul-first into a mad doctor's practice of dangerous
and degrading conversion therapy.

Chapter One: "Dummy" and Chapter Two: "Canine" are
available now. Visit the Paradigm Shift Productions website
for more information.

Presented illustration by Remi Lavičkova.